Death in Practice

Death in Practice

HAZEL HOLT

First published in Great Britain in 2003 by
Allison & Busby Limited
Bon Marche Centre
241-251 Ferndale Road
Brixton, London SW9 8BJ
http://www.allisonandbusby.com

A catalogue record for this book is available from the British Library

ISBN 0 7490 0665 X

Printed and bound in Ebbw Vale,
by Creative Print & Design

HAZEL HOLT was born in Birmingham and educated at Cambridge University. She worked as an editor, reviewer and features writer before turning to fiction. She currently lives on the edge of Exmoor, near Minehead with her husband. Her life is divided between writing, cooking and trying to keep up with her Siamese cat, Flip.

I would like to thank the members of my local veterinary practice for their help and also to point out that nothing like this ever happened there.

For Nat, Ant and Iain

Chapter One

"You let those animals rule your life," Anthea said, leaning on the worktop and watching disapprovingly while I cut up some cooked chicken. "They're thoroughly spoilt."

"I know," I said defensively, "but Tris is an old dog now and can't eat tinned food, and Foss is so picky – if I open a tin for him I always have to give half of it to the birds."

"Kathy's just the same," Anthea went on, now launched on a familiar theme, "always been silly about animals, ever since she was a child – cried herself to sleep night after night when that wretched tortoise died. But even so I never thought she'd end up working for a *vet*!"

Anthea's younger daughter is an assistant at our local vet's, something her mother regards as "the waste of a good education", unlike her older sister who is not only married with two children (thus providing grandmother fodder) but also head of the physiotherapy department of our local hospital.

"Jean has really *got* somewhere already and there's no saying where she may end up. But Kathy's stuck in that dead-end job – I mean, where will it lead? Nowhere!"

"But she's happy," I said, placatingly.

"That's as may be," Anthea said austerely, "but she ought to be looking to the future."

"She's still young!" I protested.

"She's thirty-five," Anthea replied, "and she hasn't even got a steady boyfriend."

"Thirty-five's nothing now," I said, "not like in our day."

"*Nothing's* like it was in our day, more's the pity!"

"I agree with you over lots of things, but, from what I can gather, it's much more fun being a thirty-something nowadays than it was when we were young."

"Oh *fun!*" Anthea said. "Life's not about fun!"

"I suppose not," I said meekly.

As my friend Rosemary always says, "Anthea is a good soul, kind-hearted and generous to a fault, and one of my dearest friends, but one must *always* remember that she has no sense of humour."

"I don't know what she does with herself," Anthea said, "she never seems to *go* anywhere. Just sits at home in that flat of hers."

Anthea has always resented the fact that Kathy, although unmarried, wanted a place of her own and had taken what her mother described scornfully as "that poky little place down by the railway station". It is, in fact, a perfectly pleasant flat in a converted Edwardian house, by the station admittedly, but also overlooking the seafront and very nice too.

"But she sings with the Light Opera Group doesn't she? Thea said how good she was in *The Gondoliers*."

"Oh the Opera Group," Kathy said dismissively. "She'll never meet anyone there – just a lot of women and all the men are married."

"Perhaps she just enjoys singing," I suggested.

"And another thing," Anthea continued resentfully. "Jim and I hardly ever see her. She used to come to Sunday lunch, but now she just makes excuses all the time."

I reflected that if Anthea went on and on to Kathy

about her single state it wasn't surprising that she avoided her parents.

"Talk about Mrs Bennett and marrying off your daughters," I said to Rosemary when I reported the conversation. "Anyone would think we were living in the nineteenth century, not the twenty-first!"

"Well," I said soothingly to Anthea, "I suppose we can't lead their lives for them."

"It's all very well for you to say that. Michael's married – such a nice girl, Thea – *and* you have a beautiful granddaughter."

"You have two grandsons," I pointed out.

"They're wonderful, of course and I'm devoted to them, but I would have liked a granddaughter. If only Kathy..."

Fortunately Foss chose this moment to appear in the kitchen and jumped onto the worktop, poking his nose inquisitively, as he always does, into whatever happened to be there.

"Sheila! Surely you don't let him do that!" Anthea cried as Foss tentatively put his paw in the sugar bowl.

"Of course not!" I said mendaciously as I scooped Foss up and put him down on the floor.

"Bad boy!" I said in what I hoped was a severe manner. Foss gave me a look of contempt and stalked off into the hall.

This little episode luckily diverted Anthea's mind from the iniquities of her younger daughter and she reverted to the real reason for her visit.

"Now what about that committee meeting? You really must come – I need you to keep Maureen in order."

Maureen Phillips is a meek woman who had once

been moved to disagree with one of Anthea's suggestions and who has been, consequently, branded by her as a red revolutionary who has to be kept down at all costs.

"Oh dear I don't think I can," I said. "I said I'd babysit for Thea and Michael that evening. But, really, I'm sure you're more than capable of controlling Maureen."

"Well that is a nuisance – Marjorie's busy too. Honestly, I can't imagine why people say they'll *be* on committees if they never turn up for meetings."

Ignoring the unfairness of her comments (I seem to spend a great deal of my life sitting around tables being bored out of my mind) I did my best to soothe her.

"Do have a cup of coffee," I said.

But Anthea, probably with the memory of Foss's dark paw in the sugar bowl, declined and, gathering up her belongings, went away to chivvy someone else.

As it happened I saw Kathy the very next day. Foss, in unheeding pursuit of a rabbit, managed to tear his back leg quite badly on some barbed wire and when I phoned they said to bring him in straight away. Unlike my dog Tris, who regards the vet's as some sort of unspeakable gulag, Foss doesn't mind it at all. Like all Siamese he obviously thinks that any attention is better than none and all the girls there respond to his blue-eyed charm.

"Poor boy!" Alison, one of the junior assistants, said as she removed him tenderly from his carrying cage, "what a nasty cut. I'll get Kathy to clean it up before Diana sees it."

"Isn't Simon here?" I asked Kathy as she carefully wiped round the wound. "He usually sees Foss."

"Oh, Simon's left. He's gone to set up on his own at Newton Abbott. Diana's taken on a lot of his patients. But Keith's still here, and Ben."

"Are you getting anyone else? It's such a large practice – I mean, Ben mostly deals with horses and farm animals, doesn't he?"

"Yes," she seemed to hesitate, "yes, we are getting someone else." She looked around to see if anyone was within earshot. "As a matter of fact they're taking on a new partner. You see Simon had put a lot of money into the practice and, now he's gone, they've had to find someone who can do the same."

"I see."

"There was a bit of a cash-flow problem – " She broke off. "I shouldn't be telling you this – please don't say anything."

"No, of course not. Well, I'll be interested to see the new partner. What's his name?"

"Malcolm Hardy."

"Really? I used to know his father – at least, he was a friend of my parents. There was certainly a lot of money there!"

Just then Diana came in and said I should leave Foss there while his leg was treated.

"It's a nasty tear," she said. "I'll have to give him a light anaesthetic, so come back this afternoon, about two o'clock."

As one always does, I fretted at the thought of Foss having an anaesthetic. Of course I knew he'd be all right but, although he's very strong, he's not a young cat, so, in my anxiety, I was back at the surgery quite a bit before two.

"He's fine," Kathy said, "but Diana just wants to

have a word before you take him home. She won't be long if you don't mind waiting."

Relieved, I sat in the waiting room which, since surgery didn't begin until three o'clock, was empty. I inspected the notices on the board. Flyers for dog-shows and sheep-dog trials, advertisement for organic dog-foods, along with the personal cards wanting homes for kittens ("two beautiful tabby boys and a sweet tortoiseshell girl"), dogs ("cross-bred lurcher, good with children") or horses ("hunter, 17 hands, quiet to ride and box"). Then I settled down with a copy of *Hello!* magazine, which I greatly enjoy but never actually buy.

I was distracted from the lush description of the wedding of a minor European royal by the sound of voices raised in one of the consulting rooms. The door was slightly open and I heard Diana say sharply, "No, that's quite unacceptable."

Another voice, male and one that I didn't recognise, said, "Well those are my terms, take them or leave them. But I think you're going to have to take them, aren't you?"

"But we need Ben."

"Not if we get rid of the farming side. I thought I'd explained – the obvious way to go is with the small animals. That's where the money is."

"But..."

"And now Dexters' are packing up we'll have all their clients. No, Ben Turner will have to go."

"But he's been part of the practice for years."

"He's getting past it anyway. Spends half his time gossiping and drinking tea with hill farmers who use us about twice a year. No, there's no room for sentiment in business, it's simply not economically viable."

"He's on a three month contract."

"OK. That'll suit us fine – give us time to build up the profitable side of the business and then, in due course, we can get a young trainee to do some of the routine stuff – it'll cost us less that way."

"I can't persuade you to reconsider, Malcolm?"

"It's the sensible way to go, you must see that. Anyway, the fact remains that the decision is now mine to take."

"Very well, if that's what you say. You will have to tell him though."

"No problem. Right then, now we've got that settled I'll be off. Tell Turner I want to see him tomorrow morning – ten-thirty. OK?"

There was the sound of footsteps and then silence. After a few minutes I heard Kathy's voice.

"Oh Diana, Mrs Malory's here to collect her Siamese... Diana, are you all right?"

"Yes," Diana's voice was muffled as if she'd been crying. "Yes, I'm all right. Just give me a few minutes and I'll be along to see her."

I quickly moved over to the far side of the waiting room so that Diana wouldn't know I'd overheard her confrontation with Malcolm Hardy. When she appeared she looked more or less her usual self though her manner was, understandably, abstracted. She brought Foss through in his carrying cage and said, "He's still a bit dopey from the anaesthetic, but he's done very well. Just give him a tiny bit of fish or something light to eat, but he may not want anything. Don't let him out for a few days and I think you'd better put a plastic collar on to stop him chewing the bandages. It was quite a deep wound – I had to staple it." She smiled slightly at my expression. "That's what we do now instead of stitches. Anyway, try and keep the dressing on and bring him back for me to see the day after tomorrow."

"He's all right?"

"Yes, don't worry. Oh, and I've given him a shot of antibiotic, just in case."

"Thank you so much." I looked down at Foss now sitting up in his cage, pleased to be the centre of attention. "He seems to be recovering."

"Yes, he's fine. The girls will give you a collar for him."

She spoke absently now as though her thoughts were elsewhere and so I went away to find Kathy.

I knew from the start that putting a collar on Foss (they look like a sort of plastic Elizabethan ruff and are meant to stop the animal getting at any wound) would be difficult. I finally got the wretched thing fastened around his neck with Foss bellowing his horror and disapproval but then, having decided that he couldn't see over it he started walking backwards, bumping into things and miaowing piteously. Tris, who always ostentatiously avoids Foss when he comes back from the vet smelling of disinfectant, suddenly appeared and, appalled at the apparition before him, began barking madly. After a few minutes of this I decided that the dressing would have to take its chance and I took the collar off. Foss gave me a cold, reproachful stare and went into the kitchen, where he polished off the chicken remaining on Tris's plate and complained loudly until I gave him a large amount of fish, after which he went to sleep on my bed for the rest of the day.

I made myself a strong cup of tea and collapsed into a chair. Only then did I begin to think about the conversation I had overheard. Poor Diana Norton was certainly going to miss Simon – indeed we all would. Not only was he a brilliant vet, but he was also kind, considerate and very good at dealing with anxious animal owners. Malcolm Hardy, on the other hand, sounded (from what I had heard today) thoroughly disagreeable. I could only suppose that no one else had been found with a suitable amount of money to put into the practice. It also seemed as if he had a controlling share and was able to do whatever he liked, such as getting rid of Ben Turner. I could understand why Diana was so upset. She's very loyal and Ben is a nice, capable middle-aged man who's been with the practice for years. For a moment I thought of leaving the practice as a sort of protest, but, as Malcolm Hardy said, Fred Dexter – the only other vet in Taviscombe – has just retired and there's nobody else this side of Williton. I was also sorry for Keith, the junior vet, and for Kathy and the other assistants. If the way I had heard him speak to Diana, who was after all a partner, was anything to go by, Malcolm would be even more unpleasant to those he thought of as underlings. All this would give Anthea more ammunition in her campaign of disapproval. Perhaps, indeed, it might be a reason for Kathy to leave. But then, if she did, what else could she do, in Taviscombe at any rate? She was a trained veterinary assistant, but there was no other practice here for her to go to.

"Anthea will like it even less," I said to Rosemary

the next day, "if Kathy goes away. She was cross enough about her getting a flat of her own, but at least she's still in Taviscombe."

"Oh, I don't think she will. Kathy's a quiet little thing and I expect she'll just keep her head down and put up with things."

"You're probably right," I agreed. "I've often thought it's extraordinary how someone as shy as that can get up on stage and sing quite big parts with the opera company."

"Don't they say that shy people make the best actors because then they can lose themselves in their parts? Anyway Kathy's got a lovely voice and she always looks as if she really enjoys singing."

"I believe they're doing *Iolanthe* next," I said, "and Kathy's playing Phyllis, which is really the second lead."

"I know, Anthea told me. She was pleased as Punch though she always pretends not to think anything of Kathy's singing."

"Oh she's devoted to her really, it's just that she wants Kathy to be as *she* would like her to be. Thank goodness I never had a daughter – I expect I'd have been just the same. With Michael, though, he just went his own sweet way!"

"Jilly was too strong-minded for me," Rosemary said affectionately. "I could never have influenced her if she didn't want to be influenced. Perhaps," she said sadly, "I should have tried harder with Colin."

Rosemary's daughter Jilly (married with two children) lives near at hand in Taviscombe and is very close to her mother. Colin (divorced and childless) has always been remote emotionally and, now that he's living in Canada, is equally remote geographically,

"Colin will be all right," I said, as I've said many times before when Rosemary fretted. "He's always lived in a world of his own – lots of academics do – and I'm really sure he's happy in it."

"Yes, of course, I know you're right, it's just... oh you know!"

"I wonder," I said thoughtfully, "why there aren't more great works of literature about mothers worrying – it's a universal experience, after all, and one to which a lot of bosoms would return an echo. It's a pity Shakespeare wasn't a woman – he'd have done it rather well, but, being a man, I don't suppose it occurred to him. I wonder if Mary Arden worried about him. I bet she did when he went off to London to be a strolling player."

"I'm sure Anthea worries about Kathy," Rosemary said. "All that disapproval is only because she frets about her."

"I wonder what Malcolm Hardy will be like to the pet-owners?" I said. "He can hardly speak to them like he spoke to Diana – not if he wants to keep them that is."

"Well," Rosemary said firmly, "if he's unpleasant to me or either of the dogs, I'll go to Webbers in Williton, however inconvenient it is!"

Chapter Two

Actually, when I took Foss back to have his dressing changed, I had to see Malcolm Hardy. Diana was out on an emergency, Ben was up-country somewhere with a sick cow and Keith was already booked up. The waiting room was quite full ("Sorry we're running late – it's this emergency") and as always I was amused to see how the animals reacted to this unnatural situation. A large, ferocious-looking Alsatian was cowering under his master's chair trembling and uttering little whining noises. He was being regarded with some scorn by a smug little toy poodle who sat on her mistress' knee well above the hoi polloi on the floor below. One cat was complaining loudly at the indignity of being confined in a small basket, while another had turned its back on the whole proceedings and had gone resolutely to sleep.

Foss, sitting bolt upright in his cage surveyed the scene with his usual interest and smirked complacently when one of the other cat owners commented favourably on his beauty and behaviour.

The door of one of the consulting rooms opened and a middle-aged woman carrying a Shi-tsu came out. I heard a man's voice behind her saying, "She'll be *perfectly* all right now. Just continue with the lotion and bring her in for me to see next week..."

The woman turned and made some sort of farewell remark and came into the waiting room to make her new appointment. I heard her at the desk saying to Alison, "*Such* a charming man, I feel he really *understands* animals!"

Alison gave a grim little smile and busied herself with the computer.

When my turn came I was quite eager to see this phenomenon. Malcolm Hardy, tall and good-looking with dark curly hair and very blue eyes, advanced towards me with hand outstretched. That, somehow, put me off him for a start. He took Foss out of his cage saying, "He really should be wearing a protective collar – did no one give you one?"

"He wouldn't keep it on," I said stiffly. "Anyway, he hasn't chewed his bandages or anything. He's really been very good."

He didn't say anything but gave me a superior smile which quickly disappeared when he took off the dressing and Foss gave a low growl, something I'd never heard him do before.

"Perhaps you'd better hold him," he said as Foss struggled (something he never did with Simon) "while I look at this leg."

I held Foss, stroking him to keep him calm while Malcolm Hardy put on another dressing and gave him an injection. Then he quickly bundled Foss back into his cage and slammed the door shut, almost (as I said to Rosemary) as if he was a dangerous wild animal.

"There," he said, "*now* he'll be all right. Just you make sure he wears that collar!" He gave me what I imagine he thought was a boyish smile. "And bring him back to see me in another three days."

He held out his hand again. I reluctantly shook it and made my escape.

I went over to the desk to make the appointment. "Three days time," I said to Alison. "With Diana please, and, if she's not free, with Keith."

"Not with Mr Hardy?" Alison asked.

"*Not* with Mr Hardy," I said firmly.

"Never with Mr Hardy!" I said to Rosemary when I reported back to her on my visit. "You know how good Foss has always been at the vet's. I remember Simon saying he could never listen to Foss's heart properly with his stethoscope because he was always purring so loudly! He's never growled at anyone before. I'm sure that wretched man hurt him when he took off the dressing."

"So you didn't care for Malcolm Hardy," Rosemary said smiling.

"Sorry, was I going on? No, but really, I'm sure you'll agree when you see him. That smug and superior manner – what I can only call *smarmy*. I suppose it goes down with some people – well I know it does – but not our sort of person at all."

"Oh dear, what a shame. And Simon was so marvellous."

We were both silent for a moment considering our loss.

"You can tell the rest of the staff can't stand him either," I said. "Oh well, we'll just have to see Diana or Keith in future, but it won't be the same."

I came across another disagreeable aspect of Malcolm Hardy's character a few days later. I was in the pet shop buying a new collar for Foss (he loses them at the rate of one a month) when I saw Ella Wilson. Ella is notable in Taviscombe for taking in stray cats and dogs. She is most persuasive and usually manages to find homes for them, but the old and injured ones whom nobody wants she keeps and looks after with love and devotion. When I last enquired she had fourteen cats and two dogs living with her in the small house on the outskirts of the town. We all rally round with tins of cat food and bags of cat litter, but I know that looking after them all, and the strays she takes in temporarily, stretches her very limited resources to the utmost.

"Hello Ella," I said. "I haven't seen you in ages. How are you?"

She shook her head but didn't reply for a moment and I noticed that she looked very drawn and weary.

"Oh Sheila," she burst out. "I'm so worried."

"Why? What's the matter?"

"You know how wonderful Simon and the others were about looking after my cats and never charging – well, now this new man's come they say they can't do that any more."

"No!"

"I saw this man – Malcolm Hardy is his name – and he was really unpleasant. Said they weren't a charity – well, I know that of course, but... well..."

"And Diana?" I asked, "what about her?"

"She was very upset, but she said there was nothing she could do about it. Apparently he has the say about what happens there now. Honestly, Sheila, I don't know what I'm going to do. Poor little Mitsi has a tumour – Simon said it's benign but it needs to be operated on. I'll have to find the money somehow but, as you know, I only have my small pension..." Her voice trailed away again.

"Oh Ella, I'm so sorry. Look, let me pay for Mitsi."

"Oh no, I couldn't let you do that! No, I'll manage this time, but it's the future I'm so frightened of."

"I suppose it's only what we should have expected," I said to Rosemary later that day," but poor Ella, she's at her wits' end."

"She does such marvellous work –" She broke off and then said excitedly, "I tell you what – let's get up a sort of subscription list to raise money for her. There must be heaps of people she's helped in some way or other. We could get them to make annual donations or something."

"Brilliant! Let me know what you want me to do. And we'll certainly let everyone know *why* we're doing this and how vile Malcolm Hardy is being!"

"Right, then, let's make a list and draft an appeal and you can do copies on your computer."

I looked a little doubtful and Rosemary laughed. "Oh go on! I'm sure you can manage that. Anyway, Michael and Thea will help you."

The response was very good and soon we had the promise of quite a substantial sum.

I told Diana about the scheme when I took Foss in for his final visit.

"What a good idea," she said. "Put me down for £25." She hesitated for a moment and then said, "Look, I'm really sorry about Ella. You know that if it was up to me we'd have continued the old arrangement."

"Yes I'm sure..."

"It's just that everything's different now."

"Yes," I said. "I understand, and the £25 will be very welcome."

She smiled gratefully. "Now then, I'll just give this young man a final shot of antibiotic and then I don't think we need to see him again. He's really healed very well, but do try and stop him chasing rabbits *quite* so enthusiastically!"

Michael and Thea were very helpful about the support scheme for Ella, as Rosemary had predicted.

"But *please*, Ma," Michael said, "for goodness sake don't go around saying these things about Malcolm Hardy or he'll be able to sue you for defamation."

"I'm only saying what's happened. He really has behaved abominably!"

"But not in any way illegally. And, after all, not everyone shares your obsession with animals. Some people would say it was only good business practice."

"Oh, very well then. Anyway, we've got a splendid lot of promises."

"We really need to set up a proper fund," Thea said, "and make it all official and then people can pay annually by standing order. Michael, could you get the papers drawn up tomorrow?"

She was interrupted by a loud wailing.

"Oh dear," Thea said, "I did hope she'd settled. She's usually so good about going down in the evening."

"Shall I go and see to her?" I asked.

"Oh would you? Then I can get on with supper."

I went into the nursery and found my granddaughter wide awake and demanding attention. I picked her up gingerly. After 30 years one forgets just how fragile a really young baby seems. As I patted her back gently she became quiet and I was pleased to find that some actions still came automatically, even after all that time. I walked up and down the room humming quietly to her, as I used to do to Michael, and gradually she fell asleep and I was able to put her into her cot, where she lay on her back with her tiny starfish hands flung up onto the pillow on either side of her face. I stood for a moment looking down at her and thinking how lucky I was and wishing, with a tinge of sadness, that Peter could have seen his grand-daughter and that my mother could have known that her great-granddaughter had been named Alice after her.

A few days later I was just coming out of the post office when I ran into Anthea.

"Oh Sheila, I'm so glad to have caught you. Have you got a minute?"

Fearful of being chivvied into another meeting of some kind, I began to formulate some sort of excuse but Anthea swept it aside.

"Come and have a coffee in the Buttery. I can come back here later."

With our coffees ("No, nothing else for me, I never eat between meals") in front of us I waited for Anthea to begin. However, unusually for her, she didn't plunge straight in but seemed to hesitate. After a moment she said, "I'm really worried about Kathy."

"Why? What's the matter?"

"I can't make it out. She's obviously upset about something and she won't tell me what it is."

"Is it work?" I asked. "That new man, Malcolm Hardy, seems pretty disagreeable. Has he been unpleasant to her?"

"Well, she doesn't seem to like him – none of them do – but I don't think he's been picking on her particularly. Mind you, now he's brought this new girl in there's been even more ill feeling."

"New girl?"

"Yes, Julie Barnes – do you remember her mother, Cynthia Barnes? She used to be Cynthia Burton, married that farmer out at Winsford. Anyway, everyone thinks she's this Malcolm Hardy's girlfriend so you can imagine they all hate her."

"Good heavens! And you think all this is why Kathy is so unhappy?"

"Oh no, I'm sure there's more to it than that."

"What does Jim think?"

"Oh," Anthea said impatiently, "you know men, they never see anything. He just thinks I'm making a fuss about nothing. No, I wondered whether you could have a word with her."

"Me?"

"Yes, she likes you – she was telling me how nice it was to see you the other day."

"It was just at the surgery..." I began.

"And you're both silly about animals," Anthea went on. "I'm sure she'd talk to you."

"Honestly Anthea, I really don't think..."

"I did think of asking Jean to have a word, but they've never been close and Jean is so busy nowadays, what with her job and Philip and the boys. You know how full young people's lives are these days!"

Widows, I reflected, are always thought to have empty lives and should therefore be grateful to be given any tasks that other people do not wish to perform in order to fill them.

"I really don't think I can just ask her what the matter is right out of the blue like that," I protested.

"Oh, you'll think of something," Anthea said airily. "You're awfully good at getting people to talk to you. Look how marvellous you were with poor Margaret Payne when her husband left her. She wouldn't talk to a soul until you had a word with her and then it all came pouring out!"

"But that was completely different," I complained to Rosemary the next day. "I've known Margaret since we were at school together, she's my generation. But although I've known Kathy since she was a child I don't really *know* her. Not enough to ask her personal questions like that."

"Anthea is the limit," Rosemary said, "the way she simply tanks over people. Still, if I was Kathy and I had a problem I'd be more inclined to talk to you than to Anthea."

"Still, I can hardly go and knock on her door and say, 'Your mother's worried about you', now can I?"

"I expect you'll bump into her, you know what it's like in Taviscombe, you're always running into people."

And, in fact, I did bump into Kathy a few days later – well it was a bit more calculated than that. I was walking Tris along by the sea when I saw a solitary figure sitting in one of the shelters just past the harbour. As I got closer I saw that it was Kathy. She was obviously lost in thought and didn't notice me approach, in fact she looked very much as if she wanted to be alone, but I thought it was too good an opportunity to miss and called out to her.

"Hello Kathy, isn't it a lovely day?"

She looked up startled.

"Oh, Mrs Malory, how are you?"

"Fine, though Tris and I have been for quite a long walk and we both need a little rest. Do you mind if we join you?"

"No, of course not." She bent and patted Tris, who rolled over to have his stomach rubbed.

"You're so good with animals!" I said impulsively. "You must find your job very rewarding."

"Oh yes – that is I love working with the animals..."

"But not the people?"

"No, most of them are very nice, it's just – well, it's all a bit different now."

"You mean Malcolm Hardy?" I suggested.

She nodded.

"And this Julie Barnes? Is she Malcolm's girl-friend?"

"We think so," Kathy said, "though I don't think they live together or anything."

"But?"

"But it's uncomfortable having her around – we all feel she's sort of spying on us, reporting what we do and say back to *him*."

"It sounds very unpleasant."

"It *is*! It used to be such a happy practice, but everything's horrible now." She spoke vehemently and I was startled by this show of feeling in Kathy, who has always seemed to me to be an equable kind of girl.

"Do the others feel the same?"

"Diana's very upset about it all – Malcolm's taken over all the big decisions and really runs the whole thing, so you can imagine how she must feel. And Keith's run off his feet – Malcolm gives him all the difficult, tiresome things to do and then keeps on at him saying that he's not pulling his weight."

"And Ben?"

"He's sacked Ben."

"I'm so sorry. What will he do? There isn't another practice in the district – will he have to move away?"

"He can't – well, it wouldn't be easy for him. His wife's ill, you see, in a nursing home here."

"I didn't know that. How dreadful for him. And what about you?"

"Me?"

"Yes, you and Alison and Susie."

"Oh Susie's gone – she said she wouldn't stand for being spoken to the way he did. That's when he brought in Julie."

"And how does he speak to you?"

"He's – well, he's not very nice. He's often quite rude and disagreeable and he doesn't allow us to do half the interesting things Simon and Diana let us do, helping with operations and so on. He says we're not trained to do them, but that's not true, we're both qualified veterinary assistants."

"It all sounds perfectly awful," I said. "Do you feel like leaving too, like Susie?"

She hesitated for a moment and then said, "Well, to tell you the truth I have been thinking of it. But, as you say there's no other practice around here – even if there was a vacancy."

"And you haven't thought of moving away?"

She shook her head. "I don't think so. I'd hate to leave Taviscombe."

"You might go to Taunton," I suggested. "A lot of your friends in the opera group live around there, don't they?"

"Yes, but they're not really my friends – I mean, I

know them quite well of course, from singing with them, but well... No, I'll just have to stay here for the moment and hope that things get better."

"What's happened to Susie, where did she go?"

"She's got a boyfriend who lives near Weymouth – she's going to work at a practice down there."

"Lucky Susie."

"Yes."

We were both silent for a while until Tris gave a little bark at a passing seagull. I gathered up my courage and said, "Kathy, is everything all right? I mean, I know it's difficult at work, but you seem very down. Is there something else?"

She stared out to sea and didn't answer for a while, then she burst out, "No – everything's awful! Perhaps I *should* get right away and start afresh, but I really don't think I can!" She was crying now. "It's all hopeless and I don't know what to do!"

"Kathy I'm sorry, please don't cry! Can you tell me what it's all about?"

She shook her head. "No, I'm sorry but I can't – there's someone else involved."

"Is it a man?"

She nodded and, taking out a tissue, began to wipe her eyes. "I'm sorry Mrs Malory, I didn't mean to burden you with my troubles."

"Don't be silly. I want to help. Can you talk to your mother? I know she's worried about you."

"No, oh no," she spoke in some agitation. "I couldn't do that!"

"All right," I said soothingly. "I do understand. But look Kathy, if you ever do feel you can talk, then remember I'm always happy to listen."

She nodded again. "Thank you," she said mechanically like a small child repeating a lesson. "I'll remember."

Chapter Three

"I felt dreadful leaving her there like that," I said to Rosemary. "She looked so pathetic."

"So it's some young man, then," Rosemary said. "Someone at the opera group I suppose. Well it must be, she doesn't meet anyone else."

"Presumably he's married – Anthea said they all are – so it's obviously hopeless, poor girl. And I do see that she couldn't tell Anthea."

"No," Rosemary agreed, "she's impatient enough with Kathy at the best of times. It isn't that she doesn't love Kathy as much as she loves Jean – more really, because in a way one always does love the most unsatisfactory one best – but she does so want her to *make* something of her life and an unhappy love affair would be the last straw."

"I know," I said sadly. "It can't help having to work with someone like Malcolm Hardy and his horrible girlfriend."

"True. I was talking to Mother yesterday and, of course, she knew all about him and his family."

"Of course," I said. Rosemary's mother, Mrs Dudley, has an encyclopaedic knowledge of everything that has ever happened to every family with a Taviscombe connection, her informants not being confined to this country but stretching out far beyond, to the utmost limits of empire.

"She says that his mother was very possessive and always saw off any girlfriend he might have had. I think she led him a pretty dance, but she died last year so he's obviously making up for lost time."

"Does your mother know anything about Julie Barnes? Does she still live with her parents out at Winsford?"

"Apparently. So she hasn't moved in with him yet."

"No, Kathy thought she hadn't."

"Mind you, that house of the Hardys' is enormous; there'd be plenty of room. I'm surprised he still lives there, rattling about on his own. Mother says he's going to put it on the market. She knows," Rosemary went on seeing my look of surprise, "because Mr Middleton who does her garden does the Hardys' as well and he's a bit worried in case whoever buys it may not keep him on."

"Oh surely they would," I said. "There's a lot of land with the house."

"They may turn it into flats, I suppose. It really is too big for one family these days. Of course people had much larger families when that house was built."

"But Malcolm was an only child, wasn't he?"

"Of the second marriage, yes. But he has a half-sister. You know, June Hardy. Runs that rather expensive nursing home on West Hill."

"Of course! I hadn't made the connection. We're both on the Hospital Friends' Committee. I hadn't realised she was related to Malcolm. She's never mentioned him."

"They don't get on, so Mother says. Of course she's much older than he is and I don't think she liked her father marrying again when her mother died. "

"Geraldine Hardy wouldn't be my idea of a perfect step-mother," I said.

"I don't think she was actively unkind to June but, from what I can gather, she tried to keep her down, if you know what I mean. And it was worse when Malcolm was born. June stuck it out for years until she was old enough to leave home and then she went off to Bristol to be a nurse."

"Oh dear, how sad."

"Well, she managed to make a life for herself; I suppose that's the main thing."

I saw June Hardy at the next Hospital Friends' committee meeting and, looking at her, I did see a resemblance to her half-brother. Like him she is tall and her hair, though now streaked with grey, had once been as dark as his. Her manner, though, is completely different. Where he has that oleaginous, patronising style, she is warm and friendly and I do see why everyone says how splendid she is and how wonderfully she runs The Larches nursing home.

After the meeting was over and we were all standing about with our coffee chatting, she came up to me and started to talk about one of the points that had been raised.

"I do agree," she started, "about trying to get more variety in the meals, but Brian Norris doesn't realise just how tight the budget is – they're performing miracles as it is. He just won't accept the facts however much I try to put them to him."

"It's certainly something you'd know about," I said, "after all the experience you've had in running The Larches. But you know what Brian's like, he never listens to what he doesn't want to hear."

"Oh well, whatever he says things will have to stay as they are, I'm afraid, for the present at least."

"I suppose we can't really have a fund-raising drive for the *food*," I said thoughtfully. "Extra library resources, a fish tank or new chairs for the out-patients waiting room, things like that are within our domain, but for something fundamental like the catering – well it just wouldn't sound right somehow, would it?"

"We do raise money for some pretty fundamental things," she protested. "That new piece of x-ray equipment, for instance, that was a splendid effort."

"Yes, of course. I'm just being frivolous – quite unsuitable at committee meetings."

She smiled. "Don't you believe it. Many's the time I've longed for a bit of frivolity on such occasions!"

She was being so friendly and nice that I almost mentioned Malcolm to see what she made of him, but then I thought better of it. What could I have said? "I see your half-brother's taken over the vet's practice and he's horrible and everyone hates him!" Hardly. Not really something one could say to a blood relation, even if they didn't get on. So I confined myself to general chat about the meeting, pleased, actually, to find someone whose views coincided with my own.

"She's such a nice person," I said to Thea as we drove to the clinic the next day. (Thea is very good about such things and positively encourages me to tag along when Alice goes for her check-ups and so forth, saying – bless her – that it helps if I do the driving.)

"I remember her quite well," Thea said. "She was friendly with my mother when I was child – she used to come to tea on Sundays sometimes, things like that. I always liked her. She was good with children –

I think she originally trained in paediatrics when she was at Southmead Hospital in Bristol. I wonder why she never married? Was there anybody, do you know?"

"Not that I know of. But she was away for quite a while. She hasn't been back in Taviscombe all that long."

"Well she's certainly done a wonderful job at The Larches. They say it's really marvellous now."

"It's extraordinary how two siblings – well, half-siblings – can be so different. She's the absolute opposite of Malcolm Hardy."

"Goodness yes," Thea said. "I *do* see what you mean about him! I took Smoke in for her injections and had to have him because everyone else was busy. He was really rough with the poor little thing. And the way he spoke to Diana – she came in while I was there to ask him something – terribly off-hand and scornful, treating her as if she was a fool, and she's a far better vet than he'll ever be, not to mention being a partner. And she was only checking something with him out of politeness because it was one of his clients."

I sat in the waiting room while Thea took Alice in to be weighed and measured and whatever it is they do to babies these days and while I was sitting there a young woman with a little boy asleep in a pushchair came and sat beside me. I thought her face was familiar and I was just racking my brain trying to put a name to a face when she spoke to me.

"Mrs Malory, isn't it? I don't suppose you remember me – I'm Tina Rogers."

"Of course! How are you Tina? It's been ages since I saw you."

Tina is the wife of one of Michael's young assistant solicitors and I've met her at various office occasions.

"Yes, doesn't the time fly?" she said. "I hadn't had William then."

"He's gorgeous! How old is he now?"

"Nearly a year – his birthday's next month." She bent over and tucked the blanket more securely round the sleeping child. "But what are you doing here?"

"I'm waiting for my daughter-in-law. My granddaughter's come for her six monthly check-up."

"That's nice."

I thought she sounded a bit wistful so I said, "I'm so thrilled to have a grandchild. I expect your parents are too."

"Well…" She hesitated. "My father's delighted of course, but I'm afraid my mother isn't able to… Actually she's in a nursing home with Alzheimers and doesn't really know me."

"Oh dear, I'm so sorry, how dreadful for you."

"Just sometimes she seems to recognise me and when I took the baby in she half knew it was something to do with her, but not really."

"That's so sad."

"The only person she still recognises is my father, and he does go to see her as often as he can, but with his work he can't visit at regular times so that doesn't help."

"His work?"

"He's a vet – I expect you know him – Ben Turner."

"Yes of course I do, but I had no idea you were Ben Turner's daughter. That's life in Taviscombe for you – everyone is always related to someone you know."

She laughed. "I know, and it can be really embarrassing sometimes!"

I said, "I was so sorry to hear that he's leaving the practice."

"Sacked more like!" Tina's voice was hard. "That Malcolm Hardy – I don't know who he thinks he is, coming into the practice like that and laying down the law. Getting rid of my father as though he hadn't been there five minutes." She turned to me and said earnestly, "He's worked hard for that practice, Mrs Malory, all these years, and this is all the thanks he gets. I couldn't believe Diana would agree to such a thing. Well, in times of trouble you certainly get to know who your friends are!"

"It is scandalous," I agreed, "but I don't suppose Diana had much choice. After all, from what I hear, Malcolm Hardy has put a lot of money into the practice and I suppose what he says goes. But it is a disgraceful state of affairs. I gather no one likes the wretched man."

"They all hate him at the practice. He's a bully and, according to Father, not a good vet."

"Well I certainly wouldn't have him for any of my animals," I said. "But what is your father going to do? Has he found something else?"

"He was offered something in Leicestershire, but it would mean uprooting my mother and leaving me and William – he'd hate that, so I don't think he'll take that job. But there doesn't seem to be anything else nearer. I know he's really desperate, though he does try not to worry me and puts a brave face on things."

"I'm so sorry, Tina."

The child in the pushchair stirred and began to

whimper and she bent over to soothe him. Thea came out with Alice and greeted Tina.

"Hello! I haven't seen you for ages. Hasn't William grown!"

They chatted for a moment until the nurse came out and called Tina in.

"How's Alice?" I asked.

"Oh absolutely fine – average height, average weight, average everything. Isn't that splendid?"

"Splendid," I said, suppressing the thought that my grandchild shouldn't be classified as average *anything* when she was obviously quite remarkable in every way.

"I thought Tina was looking a bit rough," Thea said as she eased Alice's carrycot into the back of the car and fastened the seatbelt round it.

"She's worried about her family," I said. "Did you know that her father's Ben Turner – at the vets'? "

"Really? No, I never knew."

"And her mother has Alzheimers, poor woman. Poor Ben, too, of course. It must be the most awful thing to cope with even if she's in a nursing home. And that must be costing him a pretty penny – if it's a private one, that is – so losing his job will be particularly awful."

"That wretched man Hardy has a lot to answer for," Thea said.

"He's certainly made everbody's lives miserable," I said, "and he's only been there a few weeks. Goodness knows how it will all end up."

I had the opportunity to see for myself how bad the atmosphere at the surgery had become when I called in a few days later to collect some special dog food for Tris.

There was no one at the reception desk when I went in. It was morning so there was nobody else in the waiting area though I could hear voices coming from out the back. Although I tried hard I couldn't make out what was being said but the voices were angry and suddenly a girl rushed out, past the reception desk and through the other door to the room where the animals sat in cages waiting for their operations. From the brief glimpse I caught as she dashed by, it seemed to me that she was crying. I heard Malcom Hardy's voice calling after her: "Julie, for heaven's sake stop behaving so stupidly! There's no need to be like that!"

He burst into the reception area and stopped short when he saw me. For a moment he looked nonplussed then he called out angrily, "Kathy, why is no one in reception? This is intolerable!"

Kathy came out with a cloth in her hands.

"There was an emergency – Alison had to go and help Keith with that Alsatian," she said. "Julie was supposed to be taking over out here. I'm disinfecting the pens like you told me to. You said it had to be done right away."

"Never mind that now," he said irritably. "Come and see to Mrs – er." He turned to me and said blandly, "I'm so sorry you've been kept waiting. An emergency, I'm afraid – happens in the best regulated circles." He gave me what he imagined to be an affable smile and went out.

"Well!" I said. "What was all that about?"

"Don't ask!"

"Was that the famous Julie?"

She nodded.

"I thought she was his girlfriend?" I asked, curious.

"She *was*," Kathy said. She looked over her shoulder to see that no one could overhear. "That seems to be all over. There was a terrible row yesterday and this morning they haven't spoken to each other – I think he's been avoiding her – until just now when she cornered him in one of the consulting cubicles and, from what I can tell, she really let fly!"

"Goodness."

"It's all been very unpleasant."

"I can imagine."

I would have asked more questions but Malcolm Hardy suddenly came back so I said hastily to Kathy, "I'd better have the very large bag of that Senior dog food – he does get through a lot for a small dog."

The large bag was quite heavy but Malcolm Hardy didn't help Kathy lift it off the shelf, nor did he offer to carry it out to the car for me, as Simon would have done. But, then, I imagine he had other things on his mind.

Chapter Four

We'd had a spell of really awful weather: wind and rain and very cold.

"Honestly," I said to Rosemary, "you'd never believe it's August."

"Oh, I don't know. I can remember Augusts when the children were small, sitting on the beach with them wearing my sheepskin coat because it was so cold!"

But after about a week of this things suddenly improved dramatically, really warm and sunny, proper summer weather in fact. I'd just decided that I really ought to take the opportunity to tidy things up in the garden – a lot of things had blown over in the wind or had been bowed down and snapped off by the heavy rain, so it all looked a bit of a mess – when the phone rang. It was Rosemary.

"Isn't it gorgeous," she said. "Goodness, how much better one feels when the sun shines!"

"I know, I've been feeling really miserable in all this damp and gloom. The summer's so short it seems unfair when the weather's awful."

"Exactly. I was saying to Jack the other day that it's quite ridiculous that we don't take advantage of what fine weather we do have. After all, here we are living in the most beautiful countryside in England and we hardly ever go and look at it."

"So what did Jack say?"

"What do you think! 'Yes dear' and changed the subject. All right, I suppose I did choose the wrong moment when he was trying to read some wretched report he'd brought home with him. Still, there's no reason why *we* shouldn't be sensible. So I've put up a flask of tea and the odd cake and I thought we might just go for what my father used to call A Little Run."

"Oh, I don't know – I was going to do some work in the garden..."

"Rubbish!" Rosemary said briskly. "That can perfectly well wait. It's such a marvellous day we can't possibly waste it."

"Oh all right," I agreed, happily abandoning any thought of fiddling about with bamboo canes and twine. "It *would* be nice."

"OK. I'll be round in about fifteen minutes."

The high moor looked wonderful in the sunshine, all purple and gold.

"There are masses of sky larks this year," Rosemary said. "When they did the burning so late I was afraid some of the nests would be destroyed. Shall we stop at Brendon Two-Gates?"

She drew the car up onto the grassy verge and switched off the engine.

"Oh bother," she said. "There's someone else here."

A large grey Range Rover was parked by the cattle grid gate.

"It's all right," I said. "There's no one there, they must be off walking somewhere."

"It is a splendid day for walking," Rosemary said. "Shall we go a little way down the combe?"

We set off across the heather, our shoes setting up clouds of pollen and releasing a sweet smell of honey.

"Oh, it is gorgeous," Rosemary said, "and such a brilliant day! I was right – we don't do this often enough."

We walked in companionable silence for a while enjoying the sense of space – the moors stretching away into the hazy distance and the great arc of incredibly blue sky above us. There was not a breath of wind and the sense of peace was almost palpable.

"'And all the air a solemn stillness holds'." Rosemary said. "What's that? Wordsworth?"

"I think it's Gray – 'Elegy in a Country Churchyard'."

"Well, whatever – it's true though, isn't it? That extraordinary stillness."

We walked down the hillside until we reached the stream that ran along the bottom of the combe.

"Oh look," I said, "there's a stone chat. I love the way they bob up and down."

We stood for a while watching the little bird and the dragonflies that skimmed across the surface of the water, then turned and made our way (more slowly) back up the hill enjoying the sunshine and the beauty all around us.

"Do you mind if we stop for a moment?" Rosemary asked. "I can't manage hills like I used to."

"I'll be glad of a little rest myself," I agreed. "When I go for a walk with the children now I tend to stop and admire the view rather more than I used to. Mind you, it's worth admiring."

I looked around me at the scattered sheep in the distance grazing peacefully, a group of ponies moving slowly across the sweep of the moor and the looping flight of a lark that had risen up almost at our feet and was soaring away into the sky singing its heart out.

"I must say I'm ready for a cup of tea," Rosemary said as she unlocked the boot of the car. "I'll pour it here, shall I – easier than balancing cups and things inside."

"Oh yes," I agreed. "So nice when the weather's fine and warm. Goodness, all those ghastly summer holidays – picnics in the rain, trying to pour tea with the car full of children and dogs and nowhere to put the milk!"

Rosemary handed me a cup and undid a tin. "Tell me what you think of these Bakewell tarts. I used Elsie's old recipe, and I managed to get some really good ground almonds when I was in Taunton last week."

The Bakewell tarts were very good indeed and I was just reaching for a second one when we heard voices and two people came up behind us and walked over towards the Range Rover. One of the voices sounded familiar and I turned to see Malcolm Hardy opening the rear door and putting a travelling rug into the back. The woman with him was talking animatedly and, though we were too far away to hear what she was saying, I could see that he was obviously very taken with her and trying to make a good impression. He seemed to be succeeding since she put her hand on his arm in a manner that was at once flirtatious and proprietary. Although we were not far away, they seemed oblivious of our presence and never glanced in our direction – obviously too occupied with each other to be concerned with two middle-aged women standing drinking tea beside a Volvo estate car. After a few minutes they got into the Range Rover and drove away.

"Well!" Rosemary exclaimed. "Did you see who *that* was?"

"You mean Malcolm Hardy?"

"No, I mean who was with him."

"I didn't recognise her, who was it?"

"That," Rosemary said, "was Claudia Drummond. You know, the wife of Sir Robert Drummond, the surgeon."

"Oh, the one who has that big house near East Quantoxhead?"

"That's right."

"Good heavens! What on earth was she doing out here with Malcolm Hardy?"

Rosemary shrugged. "I don't know, but he was carrying a travelling rug."

"You don't think..."

"Well, I wouldn't be surprised. She's got a bit of a reputation for taking up with younger men, and, from what I've heard, a little pastoral episode like this is just the sort of thing to appeal to her."

"She sounds ghastly. How do you know so much about her?"

"How do you think? Mother, of course."

"I wonder," I said thoughtfully, "if that's why Malcolm Hardy and his girlfriend were having that quarrel when I went to the surgery the other week." I told Rosemary what I'd seen and heard. "This Julie girl was obviously very upset."

"You do see interesting things," Rosemary said. "When *I* take the dogs to the vet's all I get is Muriel Sullivan boring on about her Border terrier's mange."

"I can see that this Claudia woman would be more attractive to someone like him than some silly little girl."

"She's a bit of a *femme fatale* by all accounts,"

Rosemary said. "Apparently she more or less wrecked Desmond Barker's marriage – he was quite besotted, wanted to marry her and everything."

"But?"

"But there was no way she was going to change her grand lifestyle for love in a cottage with a poor school-master."

"Goodness, she certainly seems to get around! I wonder how she got hold of Malcolm Hardy."

"Oh horses, I expect. She hunts and he – Sir Robert, that is – breeds them as a hobby. Plenty of excuses for seeing each other, especially when her husband spends a lot of his time in Bristol or London – he's very emi-nent, some sort of orthopaedic specialist. Mother once consulted him when she had that knee trouble."

"I wonder what he thinks about his wife's goings on?"

"He's a good bit older than she is, so perhaps he pretends not to notice. And I believe she's quite dis-creet."

"Your mother seems to know all about her."

"Well, you know Mother – she has her informants. Goodness, is that the time! We'd better be getting back. I promised Jilly I'd look after the children this evening so that she and Roger can go out to dinner. It's their anniversary."

"How long is it now?"

"Eleven years! Isn't it ghastly the way time just slips away? Delia is nine now and it only seems like yester-day when we were all at her christening – do you remember the crisis about Mother's hat?" She began packing up the thermos flask and cups. "Just you wait. Alice will be grown up before you know it!"

"That's why we really must do this again," I said. "Have lovely afternoons like this one while we can still can."

"Yes, we must," Rosemary agreed. "Mind you," she said, laughing, "we may not have the excitement of seeing Claudia Drummond and her latest conquest every time."

Life went on very much as usual. Thea, Michael and Alice went off to stay for a week with some friends who had a house in Brittany and I had Smoke to stay. This caused a bit of an upheaval since Tris and Foss, over-excited by a new young cat in the house, both reverted to kitten/puppyhood and went roaring around the house, all three playing complicated chasing games to the imminent danger of lamps, ornaments and any other object that lay in their (collective) path. It was during one of these episodes that Tris, forgetting that he was now an elderly gentleman, and leaping down several stairs at once, managed to damage his paw and sat in the hall whining miserably, while Foss and Smoke stopped dead in their tracks and sat regarding him with curiosity quite unmixed with concern.

"Oh Tris," I said, "what *have* you done?"

He tried to get up but it obviously hurt him. When I bent over and examined the paw he gave a little yelp and looked at me reproachfully.

"Poor boy," I said. "We must get you to the vet's. As for you two..." Two pairs of eyes, blue and green regarded me innocently. "Oh go and play outside!"

The only vet free to see me was Keith, a nice young man, usually full of chat but today strangely quiet and abstracted. He examined Tris and pronounced it just a strain and nothing to worry about.

"I'll give you some lotion to put on it," he said, "and because he's getting on a bit I'll give him a vitamin injection if you'll just hold him for me."

I stood stroking Tris while Keith got the syringe out of its package. He was just poised to do the injection when we heard Malcolm Hardy's voice outside. Keith lowered his arm and I could see that his hand was trembling.

"Are you all right?" I asked. "Is anything the matter?"

He tried to pull himself together.

"No, nothing, I'm fine..."

"You're not, are you? What is it? Is it something to do with Malcolm Hardy?"

He put the syringe down. "It's nothing really – it's just that we had a bit of a set-to earlier on."

"A set-to?"

"Yes, he accused me of having given too much anaesthetic to a dog he was operating on – we lost it, it died on the table – but it was his fault. The dog had a heart condition – he should have told me but he never did – and we usually use a different sort of anaesthetic in cases like that. He should have told me! He's trying to make me take the blame!"

Keith was becoming quite agitated, so I said soothingly, "I'm sure it will be all right. Everyone knows that you're most conscientious and professional."

"The owner was really upset – she'll blame me. And there's the insurance..."

"Diana will speak up for you. She knows how reliable you are."

"Diana can't do anything – *he's* in control of everything now. I don't know how much longer I can stay here! We're all in such a state, not just me – everyone. I really don't know how it's going to end."

Tris, already nervous, became agitated at the tone of Keith's voice and began to whimper.

Keith immediately bent to stroke and reassure him, then turned to me and said quietly,

"I'm sorry, Mrs Malory, I shouldn't have spoken like that, please forget I said anything."

"It's all right," I replied. "It's all right, really it is."

This reiteration seemed to reassure him and after a moment he picked up the syringe and gave Tris his injection.

"He should be all right now, but bring him back if you're worried." He stroked Tris's head again and Tris licked his hand.

"You're honoured," I said, "he doesn't do that to everyone. He obviously likes you."

Keith smiled wryly. "If being a vet only meant dealing with animals, it would be a perfect life."

"That's the important bit," I said. "Just don't let the other bits get you down."

When I got home the cats, as usual, refused to have anything to do with Tris because of his vet's smell, so I lifted him up onto the sofa and we sat companionably side by side sharing the Garibaldi biscuits I was having with my tea. I was saddened by Keith's outburst. He was usually a cheerful, composed young man, excellent at his job, kind and careful with the animals and reassuring with their owners. To see him reduced to that state was upsetting and a sad indication of just how badly things had gone wrong with the practice.

The more I saw and heard of Malcolm Hardy the more I disliked him. He had ruined the happy, friendly atmosphere and alienated all the staff (even the wretched Julie) and I didn't see how the situation could possibly be retrieved. The fact that there was no other practice in the neighbourhood that unhappy clients could go to meant that the tension would inevitably get worse until – well, until what? Like Keith, I couldn't imagine where it would all end.

I met Anthea the next day when I was wandering aimlessly round the Library.

"Have you had a word with Kathy yet?" she asked, coming straight to the point as she always did.

"Well, yes, in a way. That is, I saw her the other day, quite by chance when I was walking Tris along the seafront and she was sitting..."

"Yes, yes," Anthea interrupted. "So what did she say? Did you find out what's the matter with her?"

"I think it's just that she's unhappy at work. This new man, Malcolm Hardy, does seem to be really awful; he's reduced Diana to tears and poor Keith – the junior vet – is really upset. And he's sacked Ben Turner, who's been there for years."

"Has he been picking on Kathy?"

"No – well, not specially. He just seems to have been beastly to everyone, even Diana."

"And you really think that's what's been bothering her?"

I hesitated for a moment. As a parent I knew how Anthea must be feeling, but then I had promised Kathy I wouldn't say anything to her mother about what appeared to be an unhappy love affair. I know

Anthea loves both her daughters very much, but in a situation like that she would go charging in, demanding to know who the young man was and generally upsetting Kathy, who is a sensitive soul, very much.

"Yes," I said. "I think so. The atmosphere there is really poisonous – I'm not surprised that Kathy hates it. But, as they all know, there's nowhere else for them to go in Taviscombe and none of them want to move away."

"I should think not!" Anthea exclaimed indignantly. "Taviscombe is Kathy's home – there's no question of her moving. Jim wouldn't hear of it and neither would I! Oh well, at least she's got her Operatic Society. That should take her mind off things and cheer her up a bit. Did I tell you she's singing Phyllis in *Iolanthe*?"

I smiled. "Isn't that splendid! I'm so looking forward to seeing it. How are the rehearsals going?"

"Oh, I don't know, she never says. But then, nobody ever tells me anything!" She looked down at the book I had taken from the shelves. "*Corpse Diplomatique* – a thriller! That's a bit low-brow. The last thing I'd expect an intellectual like you to be reading!"

She left me with my usual mixed feelings; affection and exasperation in equal measure.

Chapter Five

Actually it was Anthea who rang me, several days later, with the news.

"You'll never believe it – Malcolm Hardy's dead!"

"What?"

"He's dead. Malcolm Hardy. Kathy's just rung me."

"Good gracious, what was it? Did he have an accident? Where did it happen?"

"It was at the surgery. Apparently he collapsed and they took him to the hospital, but he died soon after."

"How dreadful. Do they know what caused it?"

"Kathy didn't say. She was really quite upset. It's not surprising – I know he was really unpleasant, but, well, a sudden death like that..."

"It must have been awful for all of them," I said to Rosemary when I rang her to pass on the news. "*Especially*, in a way, because they all hated him. I mean, they may have wanted him dead – not in those words exactly, but wanting him not to be there – and then to have him die suddenly like that – well!"

"Worst kind of wish fulfilment," Rosemary agreed. "Still, even if they do feel uncomfortable about it, I bet no one will grieve for him."

"Except Claudia Drummond perhaps."

"Goodness yes. I wonder if she knows?"

"Soon will. I expect it will be in the obituaries in the *Free Press* on Friday."

It was indeed in the local paper, not just in the obituaries, but splashed over the front page in large black type: "Mystery Death of Well-known Local Vet".

Rosemary was on the phone early on Friday morning.

"Have you seen it?" she asked. " 'Mystery death' could be anything – I suppose they can't come right out and say 'Murder' until after the inquest. I haven't been able to ask Roger about it yet."

Roger is Chief Inspector Eliot and Rosemary's son-in-law, now working at police headquarters in Taunton but still (to Rosemary's relief) living in Taviscombe with his family.

"I do need some more flea stuff for Foss," I said. "I could go along to the surgery later this morning."

"Good idea. See what Kathy has to say."

But when I got to the surgery there was a police car outside and the place was shut up. On one of the doors someone had stuck a handwritten notice:

The surgery will be closed until further notice. In case of emergencies please telephone our usual number and some-one will get back to you.

As I stood reading this I heard a voice behind me.

"I might have known that *you'd* be on the doorstep!"

It was Roger.

"Oh, Roger – I just called to get some more flea stuff for Foss..."

"Of course," he said smiling. "And the fact that Malcolm Hardy has died in suspicious circumstances has nothing to do with it?"

"So there *are* suspicious circumstances then?"

"Perhaps – we don't know for sure. We're waiting for the post mortem. How well did you know him?"

"Not at all really – just as a vet, not as a person. How did he die? The papers were very vague about it."

"He collapsed here at the surgery and went into a sort of coma. We don't know yet what caused it."

"A coma? Was he a diabetic then?"

"It's a possibility; no one here seems to know, although there's no reason why they should if he didn't choose to tell them."

"I suppose not."

"Look, Sheila, I have to get on..."

"Yes, of course," I said. "Good luck with your investigations."

I stood aside while he knocked on the surgery door and was admitted by a police constable and then turned slowly away considering what he had told me.

If it was simply a diabetic coma then it wasn't a 'mystery death' after all, just newspaper hype. I hoped it *was* as simple as that. A murder investigation would be very unpleasant for everyone at the practice, especially as it was well known that Malcolm Hardy was deeply disliked by everyone who worked there. They must all be feeling very apprehensive, wondering what the result of the post mortem would be and if the whole thing would be taken further. Well, we would all have to wait and see.

Actually, though, I did have the opportunity to make enquiries myself that very afternoon. I was in Woolworths trying to find the cards of elastic, all that remained of the haberdashery department, when I saw June Hardy also apparently looking for something. She smiled when she saw me and said, "You haven't any idea where they've put the shoelaces, have you?"

"I *think* I saw them down at the end by the light

bulbs," I said, "though what shoelaces and electrical goods have in common I don't know – a great leap of the imagination on someone's part, I expect. But, June, I was very sorry to hear about Malcolm."

"It was quite a shock," she replied.

"Someone said he went into a coma," I went on. "Was he a diabetic?"

"As you probably know, we weren't on very good terms so I haven't seen him for some time. He certainly wasn't diabetic as a young man. Of course, it is something that can develop, though that's usually in later life – senile diabetes, several of my old people suffer from it. I suppose he *could* have developed it, though there's been no tendency towards it in the family. No, as far as I know Malcolm was a perfectly healthy young man."

"I see."

"There are several other causes of death that would result in a kind of coma, or what might appear to the layman to be a coma." June did like to air her medical knowledge. "Certain neuromuscular blocking agents such as ephedrine which might be inhaled or ingested would produce a similar sort of effect. However, I don't imagine *that* would be a very likely cause of death in Malcolm's case, do you?"

"No," I agreed, not having had the faintest idea what she had been talking about. "Still, I expect they'll know after the post mortem."

"Exactly. Dr Porter at the hospital will probably do it – he's in charge of forensics for our area, you know. A really excellent man, I got to know him quite well when I worked with him when we were both at the BRI in Bristol."

"Really?"

"Yes. He came to Taviscombe because his wife wanted to move down here. She wanted to be near her mother – Mrs Forster, did you know her? She used to live at Brendon Lodge, that big house on the Taunton road. I always thought it was such a pity – he was quite brilliant and could have gone right to the top of the tree if he'd stayed in Bristol, but there you are, that's life, isn't it!" She looked at her watch. "Goodness me, is that the time? I must be getting along. Shoelaces down there, you said? See you next week at the Friends' committee meeting."

"Any news?" Rosemary asked when she came to coffee next morning.

"Bits and pieces," I said, "but nothing positive."

I told her what I'd gleaned from Roger and June.

"So it could be anything," Rosemary said. "Not murder at all."

"You sound disappointed."

"Well, hardly that, but you must admit that if there was ever someone *born* to be murdered it was Malcolm Hardy – everyone hated him!"

"True. He was totally obnoxious."

"I wonder when the surgery will be open again? I suppose if he died there the police will have to examine the place pretty thoroughly. Even if it's not murder it will probably be suspicious circumstances, at least until after the post mortem and the inquest."

"I wonder what Diana will do now," I said thoughtfully. "She needed Malcolm Hardy's money to keep the place running. Who do you think inherits? There must be quite a bit; the Hardys were very well off and then there's that large house standing in enormous grounds – that site must be worth a pretty penny. You could get a small housing estate in there!"

"Oh you wouldn't get planning permission for that," Rosemary said, "but the house would make a marvellous hotel or, even better, a nursing home, and you know what gold mines *they* are in Taviscombe!"

"Perhaps June will get everything," I suggested, "and then *she* could turn the house into a nursing home. Unless there are any other relations – are there?"

"I don't know – I'll have to ask Mother. Though, of course, Malcolm may have made a will leaving it to someone we've never heard of."

Life went on and Thea and Michael and Alice came back from their holiday. Smoke went home and Tris and Foss spend hours looking for her, Foss prising open cupboard doors in case I was hiding her away somewhere. I spent a lot of time in the garden pulling up the forest of weeds that always spring up after a rainy spell and dividing plants that had spread too far in directions I didn't want them to. I was engaged in a struggle with a giant hosta (well it had been a perfectly normal sized hosta when I bought it) trying to prise it into two parts with a fork and a spade, and getting hotter and crosser by the minute, when Michael appeared.

"I thought I heard you out here. What on earth are you doing?"

"Trying to divide this wretched thing into two, but I can't get the leverage – here, you have a go!"

Michael eased the spade and fork more firmly under

the plant, gave it a heave and split the unwieldy plant neatly into two.

"There you are."

"Thank goodness – how did you do that?"

"Brute strength and ignorance. Now put away all that stuff and make me a nice cup of tea. There's something I want to ask you."

"What's that?"

"All in good time. Tea first. And biscuits, unless you've got some of that fruit cake left."

I made the tea and found some cake and we sat down peacefully in the living room. "Now then, what is it you want to ask me?"

Michael took a bite out of his piece of cake and put the plate down on the arm of the sofa, something that usually irritates me greatly, but I was so anxious to hear what it was he had to ask that I didn't say anything.

"It's something I want – well, *we* want – your opinion about," Michael said.

"Yes?"

"You remember Andrew Church?"

"That nice man who used to be with your practice? Yes, I remember him. He left to go to some high-powered place in London, didn't he?"

"That's right. He was a good chap and we got on very well. Anyway, I've heard from him recently. He's been incredibly successful – he always was a very good tax lawyer – and now he's a senior partner."

"Good for him."

Michael ate some more of his cake. "The thing is, he's asked me to join the practice."

"In London?"

"Yes."

My heart gave a sudden lurch and I felt sick.

"Well," I forced myself to sound bright and interested, "what do you and Thea feel about it?"

"It's a lot more money," Michael said, "and the chance of fairly rapid promotion – the firm is growing..."

"I see."

"But we'd be really sorry to leave Taviscombe and all our friends."

"Yes."

"And I know you'd hate not seeing us so much and missing Alice and things, but you could always come to London as well..." His voice trailed away and he was silent for a moment. "Well, what do you think?" he asked.

"I think," I said slowly, "you must do what *you* – you and Thea – want to do. It's your decision."

"It's a chance that will probably never come again," Michael said, "and now that we have Alice – well, there'll be all sorts of things – expenses – children need so much these days."

"What does Thea say?

Michael gave a rueful smile. "She says she's leaving it to me to decide. She says as long as we're together it doesn't matter where we live."

"Oh dear. So it's all up to you?"

"Yes – so you do see I'd like to know what you think."

"I don't want to prejudice you, say anything that might sway you one way or another. You have to make up your own mind. You know what you have here – the place, the people, the memories – but you also know that you'd probably have a better lifestyle with a lot more money in London. And you like London – Taviscombe hasn't much to offer in the way of entertainment – and at work you might like the excitement of a big City office. It's very tempting."

"Yes."

"But is it enough?"

"What do you mean?"

"The money, the job satisfaction, the scope London would offer you in every way. Is that what you really want? Is it enough to leave all the things you enjoy here? Or, if you stayed, would you regret it ever after if you didn't seize the opportunity?"

"Would you come to London with us?"

"I don't know – anyway, that's not the point. This is *your* life, yours and Thea's and Alice's. What would be best for them as well as you? Theatres, museums, shops, a choice of schools – you have to think of all that."

"I know."

"Of course," I said tentatively, "Thea's lived and worked in London and chose to come back here, and you did once have an offer to go there and turned it down."

"Things were different then – we only had ourselves to think of."

"True."

Michael sighed. "Oh it's all so *difficult*! I wish you'd tell me what you really think."

"Darling, how can I! You know perfectly well that I don't want you to go, but I don't want that to influence you if it would really be to your advantage."

We went round and round in conversational circles for a while until Michael had to go.

"I've got to let them know by the beginning of next week," he said. "I'll ring you as soon as we decide anything."

I rang Rosemary straight away, badly needing her particular kind of sympathy.

"How awful for you!" she said. "How can you possibly say what you think!"

"I just want them to be happy really, it's not just selfishness – well it is, of course. I'd be miserable if they went. It's just that I honestly don't think they *would* be happy in London, however much money they had. But I can't say that, can I?"

"I know."

"When I think how blithely I suggested that Kathy might move away if she was unhappy here – it's always different when it's your own child."

"In a way, it's not so much the children as the grandchildren," Rosemary said.

"That's true. I was perfectly happy when Michael was away at Oxford and I've been very lucky to have had him here in Taviscombe for so long. I mean, look at Judith, her only child's in Australia! No, it's just that it would so hard, after longing for a grandchild, not to see Alice growing up..."

"When Roger moved to Taunton I was terrified they'd all have to go – I mean, Taunton's no distance, but it would have meant that the everyday contact would have been lost and I'd have hated that."

"That's just it – you don't have to *see* them every day, or even phone them – it's just to know that they're there, near at hand."

I didn't expect to sleep well that night and put off going to bed at my usual time. The animals with their inbuilt clocks were getting restless, so eventually I settled them in the kitchen and was just putting the cushions straight on the sofa when the phone rang.

"Sorry it's so late," Michael said "but I thought you'd like to know. We've decided to stay."

"Oh darling!"

"We both wanted Alice to grow up in Taviscombe, where we grew up," he said. "It sounds sentimental, but there you are. Besides," he added, "we'd never find such an amenable babysitter in London. Good night. Sleep well."

Chapter Six

In the first flush of my relief (I found I had developed a tendency to go around the house singing, much to Tris's disapproval) I didn't think much about Malcolm Hardy and the causes of his death until I happened to run into Kathy one morning by the cashpoint machines in the bank. I was immediately struck by how different she looked – relaxed and smiling – quite unlike the unhappy woman I had seen down by the seafront.

"Hello Kathy," I said. "Fancy seeing you here. Is the surgery still shut?"

"No, we're open again – it's my day off."

"In that case come and have a cup of coffee."

She hesitated and then said, "Yes, I'd love to."

"I'll just get some money. That is if I can remember my PIN number – I've just changed my card and they've given me a new number."

I managed to extract my money (at the second attempt and after a hostile message from the machine) and we settled ourselves down at a table in the Buttery away from the noise of the coffee machine.

"So how's it going?" I asked. "I know I shouldn't say it, but it must be much easier for you all without Malcolm Hardy to contend with."

She nodded. "That part is wonderful. But the trouble is that now the police seem to think he didn't die from natural causes."

"Really? Why's that?"

"Something to do with the post mortem. It's all rather complicated but apparently they found insulin in the body, even though he wasn't a diabetic."

"How extraordinary – I mean, it's not something you'd take by mistake! It must have been a massive dose to have killed him."

"Well no, it wasn't. That's the odd thing."

"So what did?"

"He suffered from high blood pressure and was taking beta blockers – Propranonol, I think it was, and when that's combined with insulin it's often fatal. They found traces of alcohol as well and they say that that made things even worse."

"Good heavens! I do see what you mean about it being complicated."

"Well there's got to be an inquest, of course, so perhaps they'll sort out what actually happened then."

"As I said, the insulin can't have been an accident, can it? And it would be a peculiar and very unpleasant way to commit suicide. So that leaves..."

"Murder." Kathy said bluntly. "Yes, we've all been over it again and again and that does seem to be the most likely answer."

"Oh dear."

"It's very awkward. We all loathed him but in those circumstances we can hardly say so, even to each other."

"Yes, I can see that." I stirred my coffee thoughtfully. "Does anyone know how it happened – whatever it is – or when?"

"It was in the afternoon. He went out for lunch and came back quite early – around two, I think, anyway, quite a while before surgery at three. We usually have coffee then because most of us bring sandwiches for lunch. Alison took in his coffee about a quarter of an hour later and then, when she went to collect the cups just before three, she found him. He'd collapsed so she called Diana who tried to revive him, but she couldn't so she called an ambulance and they took him to the hospital. They say he was in a sort of coma and he didn't come round before he died."

"How dreadful. So what did you do at the surgery?"

"We didn't know what to do, actually. People were arriving for their appointments, so we just sort of carried on. Fortunately Malcolm didn't have any appointments himself that afternoon so that helped a bit, but as you can imagine it was all a bit difficult. Then at about five o'clock the police came and said we had to close the surgery. They sealed off Malcolm's room with tapes and things – there aren't any locks on the consulting room doors – and started asking us questions."

"What sort of questions?"

"Oh just ordinary things. When did we last see Malcolm, did he seem all right, did anyone call to see him – things like that. Then they sent us all home and said the surgery had to be closed and they'd let us know when it could be opened again. Diana stayed behind to check all the appointments on the computer – it would have been much easier if we'd still got the old appointment book. She was going to ring everyone and tell them not to come."

"I saw there was a notice on the door about emergencies," I said.

"Oh yes – Diana was having all those calls re-routed and she and Ben were going to cover them."

"How lucky Ben was still with you."

"Yes, we'd have been lost without him. He was marvellous."

"He was there, then, when it happened?"

"Yes – he'd called in to collect some more vaccines before his next call out at Exford. So he was able to help Diana get Malcolm off the floor and onto a couch and try and resuscitate him."

"Good for Ben. Does this mean that he won't have to leave now?"

"No one's said anything, but I don't think Diana ever wanted him to go. "

"That's good then. And I imagine that, in spite of the circumstances, the atmosphere is much better now?"

"Oh yes! Almost back to what it used to be – though, of course, we're all a bit worried about this business and what's going to happen."

"About the investigation?"

"Yes, that too, but worried about the practice. Now that Malcolm's gone we don't know what's going to happen about the money. Will we be able to carry on?"

"Oh dear, yes, that must be a worry. But, never mind, it's a thriving practice and I'm sure there must be someone out there who'll want to invest in it – someone nicer than Malcolm Hardy!"

She smiled. "I think Diana will be much more wary this time, and, as you say, the practice is doing well, so there's bound to be some interest. That is," she said, "if all this business doesn't frighten people off and we lose all our clients."

I laughed. "I think you'll find it will work quite the other way – I predict a host of new clients all coming to gawp at the scene of the crime!"

"And it does seem to be a crime," I said to Thea

when I went round there to tea later that afternoon. "I mean, insulin, but not enough to kill him – it's all very peculiar."

"Did everyone at the practice know that he was taking these beta blockers?" Thea asked. "Someone may have given him a small dose of insulin knowing that it would react with the other drugs, but hoping that he might not be found too soon, so that people might think it was just some sort of seizure."

"That's true," I said. "Come to think of it, Kathy said that Malcolm Hardy didn't have any appointments that afternoon and it was only because Alison went in to collect his coffee cup that he was found relatively quickly. If it hadn't been for that he might well have been dead when they found him and they'd have thought he'd died from natural causes. With his high blood pressure I suppose it was always a possibility."

"Actually," Thea said, "I believe it's quite difficult to trace insulin in the body after a certain time. Was it injected or taken orally, do you know?"

"Kathy didn't say. But it couldn't have been injected, could it? Not if someone killed him – I mean there'd have been a struggle surely and someone would have heard something. But can you take it orally?"

"Oh yes, I had a cousin who did. There was some reason why she couldn't be injected – I forget what – I think she took tablets, but I suppose you could just pour the stuff into a drink or something, though I don't know what it would taste like!"

"Oh well, I suppose it'll all come out at the inquest."

Thea poured the tea and cut me a slice of cake.

"Goodness," I said, "this is a *gorgeous* Victoria sponge! I'm all right on ordinary sponges, but I never seem to be able to get these right. I don't think I cream the fat properly."

"Well, I'll never be able to manage a Dundee cake like yours!" She laughed. "It *is* nice to have people to tea now I'm not working. It makes me feel just like my mother – that was mostly when she saw her friends."

"It's a generation thing. Most young people are at work now, even after they've had children. I suppose they have to."

"Yes, we're lucky that we can manage without me having to go back."

"Of course," I said tentatively, "you'd have been much better off if Michael *had* taken that job in London."

"I know. We talked about it a lot. But I wanted Michael to be the one to make the decision – I didn't want him to have any regrets later on."

"That was very noble of you!"

"I think I'm probably a people person rather than a place person," Thea said thoughtfully. "If I'm with the people I want to be with then I think I could live anywhere – within reason. Anyway, Michael decided to stay. I'm *so* glad he did. I love it here. I mean, all my happy childhood memories are here, just like Michael's. And I did make that decision for myself once, and decided to come back to Taviscombe, to come back home."

"I need hardly tell you how pleased *I* was when Michael told me you were staying – well, you can imagine."

Thea smiled. "All's well that ends well. Will you be able to stay and help me give Alice her bath? She really loves the water now and splashes around like anything."

As if on cue Alice, who had been peacefully asleep in her carrycot beside us, woke up and began to cry, not a whimper or a little grizzle, but a full-throated, "I'm here and I want attention *now*" bellow.

Thea went over and picked her up and the crying ceased as if by magic.

"Tea time for Alice too," she said. "Have another piece of sponge while I see to her."

Since I actually *did* need some more flea stuff for the animals I went along to the surgery a few mornings later. I must confess I waited until the place was empty before I went in and found Alison alone in the reception area. We discussed the merits of the various flea treatments on offer and I made my purchase.

"It must have been pretty awful for you," I said, "finding Malcolm Hardy like that."

"Oh yes, Mrs Malory, it was really dreadful."

"What happened?"

"Well, he came back early from lunch, which was a bit surprising – I mean, he didn't have any appointments that afternoon – and he was in a filthy temper."

"Really! What about?"

"I don't know, but he was slamming about, that's the way he had when he was upset. He asked for some coffee – well, he opened the door of his room and *shouted* for it, actually – so rude! Anyway, I made him some, and that was a nuisance because he has a special sort and he likes it very black and strong. I was just going to take it in for him when Diana called me to come and hold a dog she was giving an injection to – it was very nervous and needed two people to hold it down – and when I got back he was furious that I hadn't taken it in straight away."

"That wasn't very fair."

"Oh well, he wasn't. Anyhow I kept well away from him after that, as you can imagine. But just before surgery started I was washing up the coffee mugs the others had had at lunchtime so I thought I'd better collect his. He always makes such a fuss if I leave the empty mug in his room, says it looks slovenly. I knocked but he didn't reply so I wondered if he'd gone out again – like I said he didn't have any appointments – so I went in. I didn't see him at first and I'd just picked up the mug from off the desk when I saw him lying on the floor the other side of it."

"It must have been a terrible shock."

"It was! I couldn't believe it at first. You know, when you're not expecting something you don't really take it in, do you? But when I looked again I could see that he was unconscious."

"So what did you do?"

"I called Diana and she had a proper look at him and said, 'It looks serious,' or something like that and then she went and called an ambulance."

"What did you do with the mug?" I asked

Alison looked surprised at my question. "That's what the police asked," she said. "I told them. I put it in the washing up bowl in the kitchen with the others. What with all the bother I didn't get around to washing them all up until after the ambulance had been and we were all getting back to normal – not, of course," she added, "that it *was* normal, but we didn't know that then. I mean, if I'd known it was going to be important I'd never have washed up his mug. The police weren't too pleased about *that*. I suppose they thought that the stuff that killed him – the insulin or whatever – was in the coffee and I'd destroyed the evidence. I don't know, perhaps they think *I* poisoned him."

"Oh I'm sure they don't think that," I said soothingly. "Anyway the coffee was sitting around for a bit while you were helping Diana with the dog."

"And when I was making it," Alison continued. "I had to leave it half-way because the phone was ringing out here and no one was answering it."

"Well, there you are then, anyone could have put something in the mug. If that's how it happened."

"The police seem to think so." She sighed. "Oh dear, I did think all our troubles would be over with *him* gone, but things are worse than ever now."

"So it does look as if it was someone at the surgery who killed him," I said to Rosemary when I was telling her what Alison had said. "I know he was a ghastly person and impossible to work with but surely that wouldn't be enough to get him murdered."

"I don't know," Rosemary said. "People react in peculiar ways to things. If someone was really on the edge, for whatever reason, if he did something really horrible, then that might just be enough."

"I suppose so," I said doubtfully. "I wonder what Roger thinks."

"I haven't seen him for a while and, of course, now that he's based in Taunton I don't even know if he's dealing with this particular case."

"If it is murder – and it does look like it – then I'd think he'd at least want to see the report. Anyway, if you remember, I saw him at the surgery after it happened."

"Oh yes, so you did. More coffee?"

"Just half a cup. That's fine. Incidentally, I wonder why Malcolm Hardy was in such a bad mood the afternoon he died?"

"Money? Girlfriend trouble? Or just someone who didn't jump quickly enough when he gave an order? I should think it was a pretty constant state with him."

"Mmm, I suppose so, but I got the impression that Alison thought that something in particular had upset him. He'd just got back from lunch – perhaps he'd met someone then, had an argument or something."

"Perhaps it will all come out at the inquest."

But when the inquest was held we were none the wiser.

"Such a waste of time," Anthea said. "I went with Kathy because she was told she might have to give evidence, not a very nice thing to have to do, so I thought I'd go along and give her moral support. But she wasn't called after all. The police asked for a, what do you call it? an adjournment, so that they could make further investigations, they said. Such nonsense! Surely they've had enough time to work out what happened – all those post mortem reports and so on. It's so unpleasant for those girls at the surgery having that sort of thing hanging over them all the time."

"Poor Kathy," I said. "It must be horrid."

"The police are in and out all the time badgering them with questions."

"Questions?"

"Yes, you know the sort of thing. Where were they

between two and three? Did they see any strangers hanging about? Where were the drugs and things kept? Did they see the coffee mug before Alison took it in to him? Why did Alison wash up the mug afterwards? I must say," Anthea said with some asperity, "I've *never* approved of all this drinking out of mugs. What's wrong with a nice cup and saucer, I'd like to know!"

I wondered whether Anthea felt that the abandonment of proper crockery led directly to the act of murder.

"*Autre temps, autre moeurs*?" I suggested mildly.

"As far as I can see," Anthea replied firmly, "all change is for the worse."

And really, there are times when one can only agree.

Chapter Seven

"I wonder," I said, "who will get all that Hardy money now that Malcolm is dead?"

We were out on the moor, Thea, Michael and I, having what would probably be our last picnic of the season. It was a lovely day, not as hot as summer but with, as yet, no hint of autumn in the warm air. The heather was still out, though browning in patches and the bracken was becoming brittle, a foretaste of what was to come. We were sitting on a rug in the shade of one of those hawthorn trees twisted into a fantastical shape by the winter winds with Alice propped up in her carrycot, surveying with interest the strange world around her.

"Actually," Michael said, struggling with the straps of the picnic basket, "it's held in a rather odd trust. We set it up for old man Hardy, Malcolm's father; just before he died."

"Really?"

"Yes. By then June had left home. There wasn't an open quarrel but I don't think but they parted on very friendly terms so she only got a few thousand pounds. The main estate was left to his wife for her lifetime and then to Malcolm for *his* lifetime."

"You mean he couldn't leave it to anyone in his will?"

"Only to his direct heir."

"Which he hasn't got."

"Exactly. At least, not that anyone's aware of."

"So what happens now?" Thea asked.

"In the case of Malcolm dying without a direct heir then the money would go to June if he predeceased her, which given that she was a lot older than him didn't seem likely."

"And if he hadn't?"

"Then it would all go to some distant relation of June's mother who lives, as far as I can remember, in British Columbia."

"Good heavens!" I said. "What a peculiar thing. Why couldn't he just leave it to Malcolm, I wonder?"

"I don't know. Edward – he drew up the Trust – said he rather got the feeling that the old man had in some way turned against Malcolm. He never said why, it was just a feeling. Anyway, there it is. June Hardy is going to be a very rich woman."

"Ah!"

"What do you mean – *ah*?" Michael enquired. "Oh, you mean that gives her a motive for knocking off Malcolm."

"Oh surely," Thea said, unwrapping the sandwiches and laying them out on a plate, "you can't imagine June Hardy murdering anyone!"

"She's a very determined sort of person," I said, "at least on committees she is. She'll hang on like anything to get her own way."

"Still," Thea protested, "that's not the same as actually killing someone."

"Besides," Michael said, "how could she have got into the vets' without being seen?"

"Oh that would be easy," I said. "It's all open at the back because of bringing in some of the animals that way. Beyond Reception there's a sort of open area with doors to the kitchen and other rooms leading out of it. Then there's a door into the yard and another into a sort of side alley and they're all unlocked. I know because when poor Tess had to be put down I went round the back to collect her body – they don't like to bring them through the waiting area. There's a big table just outside the kitchen and if Alison put the coffee mug down there and left it several times, like she said she did, then absolutely anyone could have put something in it."

"But surely," Thea said, "only people actually working in the surgery would have had a chance to do that. I mean, no outsider could possibly know that the mug of coffee would be there at just that moment. Or, indeed, that it was meant for Malcolm anyway."

"All the mugs have their names on them," I said. "Kathy told me that she did them with nail varnish."

"Still," Thea persisted. "No outsider would know exactly *when* the coffee would be there to be tampered with."

"I suppose not," I said reluctantly.

"So there you are then." She added pieces of pie and some delicious-looking chicken drumsticks to the sandwiches. "Come on both of you, have something to eat – it's far too nice a day to brood about Malcolm Hardy and his untimely end!"

But of course I couldn't help worrying away at the problem and when I met Roger (quite by chance) the following weekend I couldn't help raising the subject. I'd been out to get the Sunday papers, something I always combine with giving Tris a bit of a walk by the sea, and I met Roger, obviously doing the same. Fortunately Tris and their spaniel get on well together and the two of them were soon engaged in an amiable game of chasing while I was able to have a word with Roger.

"How's the Malcolm Hardy case going?" I asked.

Roger smiled. "Why did I know you were going to ask me that?" he said.

"I gather," I said casually, "that June Hardy is the sole beneficiary."

"Whatever became of lawyer-client confidentiality?"

"No, really, Roger, the Will *has* been published!"

"It's all right, I was only teasing. I know Michael is the soul of discretion."

"It's a lot of money – and I remember what you always say about money being the strongest motive for murder."

"*Do* I always say that?"

"Oh come on, you know it's true."

"Very well. But I'm afraid I have to disappoint you in this case. It couldn't have been June Hardy. She spent the whole of that day at the hospital in Taunton. Apparently one of the elderly inmates at the Larches had to go there to have an endoscopy and she was with him all the time."

"Oh."

"Exactly."

"She couldn't have slipped out somehow?"

"I gather she went for a bite to eat in the canteen, but one of the nurses – someone she used to work with – had lunch with her. Anyway, it's the best part of thirty miles away so she couldn't have got there and back anyway."

"No, of course not. Oh well, I'm glad because I like

June and I wouldn't have wanted it to be her really. It's just that she seemed to have the strongest motive."

"That's the way it goes, I'm afraid."

"Mind you," I went on, warming to my theme, "Malcolm Hardy was so vile I'm sure a lot of people are glad he's dead."

"Quite a lot of people are disagreeable, but they don't all get murdered."

"Well, somebody killed him – at least, you don't think it could have been an accident, do you?"

He shook his head. "It's all very odd, really. I mean, the amount of insulin alone wouldn't have killed him – and, in that case, why insulin? There were plenty of other things in that drug cabinet (assuming that that's where the insulin came from) that would have done the job completely."

"Was the insulin from the surgery then?"

"Unfortunately we can't be sure. Apparently Malcolm Hardy said he didn't trust any of the others to check the drugs (a sore point with them, as you can imagine) and he doesn't seem to have kept the records up to date, so we have no way of telling; but it seems likely."

"I gather it was a combination of the insulin and the beta blockers he had to take for his very high blood pressure that killed him."

Roger looked at me quizzically. "You *have* been busy," he said.

"Well, Kathy who works there is Anthea's daughter, so naturally we've discussed it."

"Naturally."

"She seemed to know about the beta blockers so presumably the others did too. Still, it does seem a risky way of murdering someone – I mean, you couldn't be really sure that they'd interact and actually kill him."

"There was alcohol as well, which aggravated the situation. He went out to lunch so he was presumably drinking then."

"But people at the surgery wouldn't have known that, would they?"

"I don't know – they might have done. His behaviour may have suggested it."

"Alison certainly said he shouted for his coffee – but I gather he did that anyway. Though she did say that he was in a specially bad mood, which *might* have been because he'd been drinking. I suppose you've no idea if he had lunch with anybody, or where? I mean, if it was in a private place the other person could have given him the insulin somehow."

"Not an easy thing to do, I imagine."

"I suppose not."

"Actually, insulin when taken rather than injected is very difficult to quantify in a post mortem. In fact, if he hadn't been taken to hospital straight away it's possible no one would have known about the insulin at all."

"And the death might have been put down to natural causes?"

"With his particular medical history, yes."

"So that's why the small amount."

"It's possible."

"Do you think that means that the murderer – assuming that there is a murderer – must have had some medical knowledge?"

"Some certainly."

"Vets would?"

"Probably."

"So it's likely to be someone at the surgery?"

"Could be."

"Roger, don't be infuriating!"

"I'm trying not to leap to conclusions. We can't be certain of that, there may be another explanation."

"But you must admit it's the most likely. And, as far as I can see nobody there had an alibi."

"There was a certain amount of confusion about that time, though, from what I can gather, that's not unusual in the hour before surgery begins."

"Yes, I'm sure that's true, so that would make it a good time for someone to put the stuff in his coffee."

"Assuming everyone knew he was having coffee then."

"Oh, they would have done. Don't you remember, Alison said he shouted for it, and he had a particularly loud voice when he was annoyed – I've heard him!"

"Well, like I say, they may all have disliked him, but presumably not enough to commit murder."

"Perhaps not – just the dislike, I mean, but someone there may have had a stronger reason."

"Such as?"

"I don't know, but it would surely be worth investigating, wouldn't it?"

"Oh, I've no doubt all that will be gone into," Roger said. He smiled. "Probably by you."

"Well..." I began, but then I saw Elaine Fawcett approaching with her two dogs. "Oh dear, I'd better get Tris – he's terrified of those two Jack Russells."

We both made a dive for our respective dogs and the conversation was at an end.

"Let me know what you find out," Roger called

as he went back to his car. "I'm sure there'll be something!"

I picked Tris up and, avoiding the marauding terriers, made my way back to my own car.

Thinking about Roger's parting remark (made, I felt sure, only partly in jest) I wondered how I could find out more about the various people who worked at the surgery.

Malcolm Hardy had sacked Ben Turner. From what his daughter said, Ben would find it very difficult to take a job away from Taviscombe because of his family. Now, with Malcolm dead, it seemed very likely that Diana would keep him on.

Diana, too, would be glad to be rid of a man who was making her life utterly miserable, though she would now have to find someone else who was prepared to put money into the practice.

Keith, a gentle, sensitive person, had also been made wretched by Malcolm Hardy's bullying, and although it was hard to think of him as a potential murderer, people do strange things when under stress.

Alison and Kathy had also been badly affected by the new regime – Kathy in particular seemed to have been taking it very badly – but obviously I could rule them out. Julia, though, was another matter. If Malcolm Hardy had broken off their affair because he was now involved with Claudia Drummond, she would be deeply resentful – well, the brief scene between them that I had overheard bore witness to that. It was possible that her expectations had been high, marriage even. A rich man like that would be quite a catch for the daughter of an up-country hill farmer, and, unlikely as it might seem to me, she was probably in love with him. But would that make her want to kill him? A woman scorned and all that.

Looked at rationally like that, it didn't seem likely that anyone at the surgery, however much they might have hated Malcolm Hardy, would coolly and carefully (for that's how it had been done) plan his murder.

"It's no good Tris," I said as I brushed the worst of the sand off his paws and sat him on his rug on the back seat, "it really doesn't seem very likely."

Tris, feeling that some sort of response was demanded of him, put his head on one side, regarded me fixedly and barked twice.

"You're quite right," I said. "Let's go home."

But, as these things do, even when we got home the problem continued to go round in my head. If the people at the surgery didn't have sufficient motive and if his sister (who did) had an unbreakable alibi, then there had to someone else with a reason to kill him. Not, presumably, Claudia Drummond, who was just starting up an affair with him. Her husband, perhaps? He seemed to have been a fairly *complaisant* husband for most of their married life, but it was just possible that for him this might be one affair too far. But then he could divorce her. And, anyway, how could he have possibly administered the insulin or known what dosage would be fatal given Malcolm Hardy's medical condition? No, he had to be a non-starter.

I was going over this ground again next day with Rosemary when she came round to borrow my *River*

Café Cookbook ("Some clients of Jack's are coming to dinner on Friday – they're supposed to be terrific foodies!") and she had to agree with me.

"Of course!" I said out loud. "How idiotic of me! Apart from the Julie girl and Claudia Drummond we don't know anything about his private life. Someone like him could well have all sorts of enemies that we know nothing about."

"What sort of enemies?" Rosemary asked.

"Oh, people he's upset in some way or other," I replied vaguely.

"It'd have to be something pretty bad for someone to want to *kill* him."

"Yes – but look, perhaps in the practice he was in before he came here, he killed someone's animal, through inefficiency, carelessness, something like that. We know from what Keith said that an animal here died unnecessarily because of him. It could easily have happened before."

"The owner would be upset, of course, but don't you think murder would be going a bit far?"

"I don't know. Think of someone like Nora Lisle; she's absolutely obsessed with that spaniel of hers, it's the child she never had. *I* wouldn't want to be in the shoes of anyone who harmed it."

"Oh well, Nora Lisle's absolutely crazy, everyone knows that."

"Exactly, that's why she'd be so dangerous – she doesn't play by the rules like everyone else. There are probably lots of people like that, and if one of them thought that Malcolm Hardy *was* responsible for their death of their beloved pet, then they might do something about it."

"But how could they have given him the insulin at the surgery?"

"Not at the surgery perhaps, but there's nothing to say that he wasn't poisoned that lunchtime."

"But nobody knows who he had lunch with."

"I know. It's maddening – I'm sure it's the clue to the whole business."

"Well, I don't see how you can find out," Rosemary said, picking up the cookbook and flicking through the pages. "Goodness, this is pretty high-powered stuff. Some of these ingredients I've never even *heard* of – I don't suppose I'll ever find them in Taviscombe and I can't face going into Taunton."

"Perhaps you could adapt one of the recipes," I suggested.

"I know what would happen if I did. I've tried that before – total disaster. No, I think this is right out of my league. Oh well, back to Delia, I suppose. I could do that pepper, tomato and anchovy thing for starters, but what about the main course?"

"Fish?"

"I always overcook fish. No, it'll have to be the old faithful chicken and lemon." She thought for a moment, then she brightened up. "Do you know, I think I'm going to make Jack take us all out to dinner – that new place at Porlock Weir's supposed to be terrifically good."

"There you are," I said. "There's always an answer to every problem if you think constructively! Even," I added hopefully, "to the problem of Malcolm Hardy's murder."

Chapter Eight

There's been a glut of apples this year. Last year all I got were half a dozen small Worcester Pearmains and no cooking apples at all, but this year every single tree in the garden has been bowed down with fruit in a Keatsian abundance. Michael and Thea, bless them, helped to pick them (I'm useless up ladders) and took away half a dozen boxes full to the brim. I spent several days wrapping apples and putting them on the shelves of an old, ratproof cupboard that I keep in the outhouse for that purpose, but still there seemed to be an awful lot left. I made apple puree for the freezer and pots and pots of apple chutney so that the house smelled of boiling vinegar for days; I *lived* on apple tarts and apple crumble and Eve's pudding, but the boxes seemed as full as ever. I tried to give them away to friends, but they were in the same boat and laughed hollowly when I tentatively introduced the subject. Even holders of the produce stalls of any Bring and Buy sale I could track down gave me a polite but distinct refusal.

I had just decided to go against the frugal principles of a lifetime and chuck the whole lot on the compost heap when I thought of Kathy, living in a flat with no garden and perhaps not yet inundated with offers of surplus fruit. I rang her at the weekend when I was fairly sure she'd be at home and, to my great delight, she said she'd love to have some.

"I'll bring them round, shall I? When would be convenient?" I asked eagerly.

"Now would be fine."

I filled two large boxes with assorted apples and drove round to the flat. Kathy lived on the ground floor and had obviously been watching for me because she opened the door even before I had time to ring the bell.

"I'll just get the apples out of the car. Is it all right to park there?"

"It's fine – I'll come and help you."

I think she was slightly taken aback at the size of the boxes but nobly carried one of them into the flat.

"Just bring them into the kitchen," she said, "and put them on the table."

I looked around with interest. It was an old fashioned kitchen with a dresser full of handsome china, lots of cupboards, a large scrubbed kitchen table and a modern sink by the window, looking out onto a paved courtyard with terracotta pots still bright with flowers.

"What a lovely kitchen!" I exclaimed. "So cosy."

"I don't really like modern fitted kitchens – I get enough of that clinical look at the surgery."

She looked at the boxes of apples. "Thank you very much," she said. "They're marvellous."

"I'm afraid I brought rather a lot, but they keep very well," I said defensively.

Kathy laughed. "No, really, I love apples in all shapes and forms. I'm delighted. Would you like a cup of tea?"

"That would be lovely."

She made the tea and put out some biscuits then led the way back along the hall into the sitting-room. It was a large room, comfortably furnished (I recognised a few pieces that had come from Anthea's) with a window looking out across the road, beyond a municipal flowerbed, to the sea.

"This is splendid!" I said. "What a marvellous view."

"It is good, isn't it? And because the house is set well back we don't get tourists peering into the windows."

"I can see why you're so happy here." I looked at her. "You do seem to be happier now, Kathy. Are things better for you now? You were so miserable that day when I saw you."

She smiled. "Yes, things are better. Not absolutely all right, but better than they were."

"That's good. How are things at the surgery now? Has Diana found someone to replace Malcolm Hardy?"

"Not yet. She's taking her time, I imagine."

"Not surprising, if you think about it! How's the practice doing – financially, I mean?"

"Not too bad, as far as I can tell. We're very busy, but we can just about cope. Everyone's trying very hard, even Julie."

"Really? Is she still there? I wondered if she might have left now that..."

"No, actually she seems quite subdued, not a bit like how she was."

"Oh well, a job is still a job, I suppose."

"Yes," Kathy said slowly, "but I don't think it's just that. She seems to want to be part of the practice, to fit in, if you know what I mean."

"How strange. Still, good for you all if she's being helpful. How about Keith?"

She hesitated. "He's obviously relieved not to have Malcolm bullying him all the time, but ..."

"But?"

"I suppose I shouldn't tell you this, but I know you won't tell anyone. Poor Keith may be going to face quite a few problems."

"Really?"

"The fact is that there were several unnecessary deaths of animals and there are going to be enquiries from the owner and from the insurance people. "

"He told me about one of those, but he said it was Malcolm Hardy's fault."

"That's right. They were Malcolm's fault, but the thing is, he blamed Keith for all of them."

"Could he do that?" I asked.

"He is – he *was* – the senior partner and during the operations, apart from the two of them, the only other person present was Julie, and she'd obviously back up what he said."

"How awful!"

"It would have been. Keith would have been dismissed and he'd have found it very hard to get another reasonable job with all that in his references."

"That's dreadful! But now that Malcolm Hardy's dead, can't something be done?"

"Fortunately yes. Diana's backing him all the way and Julie's now saying that none of it was Keith's fault and Malcolm forced her to lie for him. It was quite brave of her, really, to admit that she lied. We're all very glad for Keith. He's a good vet and a really nice person."

"I wonder what brought about this change of heart in Julie?"

"I think she'd finally found out, even before he died, what a ghastly person Malcolm really was."

"That quarrel – the one I heard at the surgery that day?"

"That and several others."

"Do you know what it was all about?"

"I imagine it was because he'd dumped her. She was very resentful and he was furious at the way she was making scenes. I expect he'd have sacked her in the end."

"Well, no wonder she's doing her best to be co-operative. She must know what a bad impression she made on you all before."

"Yes. We've been glad to have her around now we're so busy, especially now she's working hard and is more reliable. A little while ago, just before she and Malcolm had that bust-up, she was always having the morning off and turning up at any old time."

Kathy picked up the teapot. "Will you have another cup?"

"No, thank you, dear, but if I may I'll just pop into your loo before I go."

"Of course. The bathroom's just down the passage on the right."

The bathroom too was slightly old fashioned with a big bath, several cupboards and a large mirrored cabinet over the washbasin. While I was washing my hands I accidentally knocked the corner of the cabinet and it swung open. As I went to close it again I saw that on the shelf inside there was an electric razor, a man's hairbrush and bottles of aftershave and hairstuff.

I moved the bottle of aftershave slightly so that I could see the label and found that it was a very expensive one, often featured in fashion magazines, which gave me a totally new and unexpected idea of Kathy's young man. Feeling slightly guilty at prying, I closed the cabinet and went back into the sitting-room.

"Well," I said as I gathered up my handbag. "I'm really looking forward to *Iolanthe*. How are rehearsals going?"

She pulled a face."Oh you know how it is – terribly difficult to get everyone together at the same time. People are so busy. Jerry – he's playing Strephon – very nearly had to pull out because his firm was going to send him to Canada for a year. We were all in despair, because it would have been impossible to find another tenor at that stage, but fortunately the people at his head office changed their minds and he's not going after all."

"That must have been a relief for you."

"Oh yes," she said, "it would have been absolutely *awful*!"

Seeing my look of surprise at her vehemence she said, "Most of my scenes and duets are with him. It would have been very difficult to do them with some-one else at such a late stage."

"I'm sure it would be. That's something I've never understood – how famous opera singers can just go and slot into a performance at any old opera house, at a moment's notice sometimes."

Kathy laughed. "The difference between amateurs and professionals."

As I made my way home I wondered if perhaps this Jerry was the man in Kathy's life. Perhaps playing young lovers on stage had sparked a real romance. It would fit. If Kathy had thought her young man was going to be sent to Canada for a year then of course she would be miserable – especially if he *was* married and would be going with his wife. And now the fact that he wasn't going after all was the obvious reason for her to be happy again. Also, I thought, perhaps naively, someone who worked for the sort of firm liable to send him abroad might well have a lifestyle that involved using expensive aftershave.

When I got home there was a message on my answerphone, an instrument Michael insisted on installing for me and which I regard as I might a coiled serpent. For some time I didn't switch it on, but Michael was so hurt I felt I had to persevere. I managed to play back this message without wiping the whole thing and found that it was from Rosemary who is as bad about these wretched instruments as I am. An agitated voice said, "Oh. Hello. Hello, this is Rosemary. Is this thing working? Mother said would you go to lunch with her on Monday? Sorry about that, but she said she hasn't seen you for a long time – you know how she is... Look, I'll ring later when you're in."

Then the line went dead and I knew that Rosemary had put down the phone and was feeling foolish at not being able to adjust to a simple piece of technology. I feel the same myself; just launching one's remarks into the void, as it were, remains for both of us an unnerving experience and one that we avoid whenever possible. I knew that Rosemary had only nerved herself to leave a message on the machine and not waited until I got home because her mother had told her to ring Right Away, and Mrs Dudley was not the sort of person whose instructions could be deviated from or modified by anyone, especially her daughter.

I immediately picked up the phone and rang.

"Oh hello," Rosemary said apologetically. "Sorry about the message, but you know how I hate those things. And I'm sorry about Mother. Only old Mrs Weston died last week – that's the second of her friends to go this year so she's feeling a bit down, well, you can imagine. So if you wouldn't mind..."

"Yes of course I'll go. It is a while since I've seen her. I was beginning to feel a bit guilty about it."

Rosemary laughed. "You see! She does that to everyone!"

"I know – but it must be awful to be really old and see your friends dropping off one by one."

"I suppose. Thanks anyway. Incidentally, I heard something that I think you'd be interested in, but I don't think I'd better tell you on the phone."

"Goodness, how intriguing. Come and have coffee – when?"

"Can't manage tomorrow, the children are coming to lunch, then Monday you're seeing Mother – so, Tuesday?"

"Fine. I'll try and possess my soul in patience until then!"

The next day, Sunday, I went to Morning Service. I don't go every week, but I knew that, since I was seeing Mrs Dudley the next day, she would expect me to give her not only a full account of the Vicar's sermon but also a detailed list of who had attended, what they were wearing and any other germane information.

St James's was quite full; well, relatively speaking. That is, a fair proportion of the central block of pews was occupied by the regulars, while those who came only occasionally perched uncertainly in the pews at the back of the church, obviously not wanting to occupy a place which might 'belong' to a regular communicant.

I sat where I usually do – three rows back, near enough to hear the Vicar's sermon (he speaks very softly – there have been several complaints about it) but not near enough to catch his eye as sometimes happens when I feel the whole force of his remarks is, uncomfortably, directed at me. Just as the minute bell was tolling, June Hardy came in and sat down in the pew in front of me. She looked harassed and slightly flustered, though that could simply have been because she had been nearly late for the service. But as we sang the first hymn ("All things bright and beautiful", omitting the third verse) she seemed to recover herself and become calmer. The vicar preached an excellent sermon on humility, illustrated by the story of Tobit, though I didn't feel that would be a subject that would appeal greatly to Mrs Dudley.

I wondered idly what it was that had agitated June Hardy and if it was something to do with her stepbrother's death. It seemed suitable that the final hymn should be "God moves in a mysterious way", and, as we sang Cowper's fine words, I wondered if the final lines ("God is his own interpreter / And he will make it plain") were a sign to me that I should stop fretting over the problem and leave well alone. But as I made my way out of the church at the end of the service I couldn't help catching up with June – who was just ahead of me – and having a word.

"Hello, how are you? Is everything all right?"

"All right – what do you mean?"

"It's just that I thought you looked a bit upset as you came in."

"Oh – well, yes, as a matter of fact I am a bit."

"What's the matter?"

"Nothing really; something and nothing, probably. There was a message for me from Edward Drayton, he's Michael's senior partner, isn't he? He wants to see me – apparently some problem has arisen, I don't know what."

"About the estate?"

"I suppose so."

"How distressing," I said. "The whole thing must have been so unpleasant for you."

"Well, it hasn't been easy. The Inspector has been asking so many questions – I know he's only doing his job, but, really, it is a very disagreeable experience and it does upset my old people to have the police around the place. A lot of them get very anxious about anything out of the ordinary. It's something that happens with extreme old age, of course, but I don't like them to be disturbed like that."

"Of course not."

"Well," she said, pulling on her gloves, "I must get on – I like to supervise their Sunday lunch myself. I always try to make it a special meal for them."

She gave me a brief smile and hurried away.

It occurred to me, as I drove home, that she must have had Edward's message on Friday. If she was still agitated by it on Sunday, then it was obviously more important to her than she led me to believe.

Chapter Nine

I was early for my lunch with Mrs Dudley and, since she always expects one exactly on time, I sat for a while in the car. Not, of course, outside the house, since there I would be visible to Mrs Dudley who always sits by the window the better to observe the world outside, but round the corner. As I sat there Anthea came by and tapped on the window of the car.

"What on earth are you doing there?"

I explained the situation and she said, "Lunch? With Mrs Dudley? Goodness, you are honoured!"

I laughed. "A mixed blessing."

Anthea leaned in at the window and said confidentially, "I know you'll be pleased to hear that Kathy seems *much* brighter now. It must have been that dreadful man, so really, although I know you shouldn't speak ill of the dead, I can't help but being pleased that he's gone."

"I think that's the general feeling."

"Mind you, it's still very unpleasant for them all at the surgery. I mean, it's awful to think that one of them might be a murderer."

"The police haven't any other leads then?"

"Oh, the police," Anthea said scornfully. "They don't seem to have any idea, except harassing those poor girls."

"Still," I said cautiously, "it's unlikely to be anyone from outside."

"I don't see why not," she replied. "Kathy said that

that man was out at lunchtime. It could have happened then."

"Would the timing have been right?"

"Oh I don't know about that sort of thing!" Anthea brushed this aside. "All I know is they don't seem to have thought about anything or anyone not connected with the practice. I'm sure a person like that must have had a lot of enemies."

I was about to agree when I caught sight of the time and realised that now I would be five minutes late. I said a hasty goodbye to Anthea and drove round the corner.

"Ah Sheila," Mrs Dudley said, "better late than never."

By way of apology I proffered the sheaf of flowers that I had brought.

"How kind," Mrs Dudley said, inspecting them. "Chrysanthemums – I always think of them as funeral flowers. However, it was very good of you to think of me. Elsie will put them in water."

Having put me in my place, as it were, she became more affable and questioned me about Michael and Thea.

"I was delighted that they called the baby Alice after your dear mother. That is what I call a *proper* name. So many children nowadays, even from quite good families, are given such unsuitable names. Tracy!" she exclaimed. "Jason! Can you imagine a respectable elderly person with a name like that?"

I was obliged to agree that I couldn't.

"It's all *fashion*, whatever they mean by fashion nowadays; pictures of half-starved girls in their underwear. I cannot believe what the world is coming to. However, thankfully, at my age I shall not be required to put up with it much longer." I made little ineffectual protesting noises which she rightly ignored. "I am only grateful that my dear father is not alive today to see what has happened to this town. Have you *seen* the way the trippers go about half naked, in shops, even in the post office?"

"I know it's awful..."

"It's an affront to common decency. I cannot think what the police are doing to allow it."

I tentatively suggested that the police had quite a lot of other things to cope with.

"Well, they certainly don't seem to have made much progress in that Hardy affair – I was mentioning it to Roger only the other day."

Unfortunately at this moment Elsie came in to say that lunch was ready and I was afraid that any information Mrs Dudley might have had would be lost. However, I underestimated my hostess's determination to pursue her chosen topic to the bitter end, and as soon as we were settled with our delicious lemon sole she continued.

"I cannot believe that anyone will grieve for that dreadful Hardy boy," she said sticking her fork with some violence into the quarter of lemon and squeezing the juice onto her fish. "Nevertheless, it has been some time since he was killed and no one has been apprehended yet."

"What did Roger have to say?" I asked.

"Oh, some nonsense about investigations being under way and alibis being checked – bureaucratic nonsense. It's perfectly obvious to me who killed him."

I sat riveted, my fork half-way to my lips.

"No! Really? Who?"

"That half-sister of his, of course. She's his only surviving relative and stands to inherit a great deal of money."

"Oh," I said deflated. "No, it can't be June. She was in Taunton all that day, she had to take one of her old people to Musgrove for an endoscopy."

Mrs Dudley, who is passionately interested in illness, was instantly diverted. "Who was that?"

"I don't know."

She made an exclamation of annoyance at my incompetence. "I expect it was Major Lister – I did hear that he was having some sort of trouble with his throat." She spread a piece of her roll lavishly with butter. "He was always a heavy smoker and see what it has brought him to."

"So you see it couldn't have been June."

"Possibly not. Unless," she added dramatically, "she had an accomplice."

"An accomplice?"

"Exactly." Mrs Dudley took a sip of her wine and looked at me triumphantly. "Someone who was in the position to administer the poison."

I stared at her in amazement. "Who on earth...?"

"Ben Turner."

"What!"

"People have seen them together – indeed I saw them myself in deep conversation the last time I was in my bank."

"But surely...?"

"And of course his wife is a patient at The Larches – Alzheimers, you know, quite tragic."

"Well, there you are," I said, "they were obviously talking about her condition..."

Mrs Dudley ignored my interruption. "The whole sad business has drawn them together. Elizabeth Turner was always a difficult woman; he can't have had an easy life. So what would be more natural," (Mrs Dudley occasionally liked to take what she would have called in other people A Shocking Point of View to establish her liberal credentials) "that he should turn to someone sympathetic at such a time."

"Well..."

"And June Hardy is a clever woman. Once she'd got him twisted round her little finger she could have got him to do anything."

I considered this view of June as a sort of *femme fatale*.

"But they're neither of them like that. I mean, Ben is a really nice man and June does such good work for the hospital."

Mrs Dudley gave what in someone less refined would have been a snort of contempt.

"June's father, Leonard Hardy, was always giving money to good causes, but that didn't make him a good man. Quite the contrary."

"Really? He always seemed quite nice when he came to see my parents."

"Not at home!" Mrs Dudley said with authority. "He was a terrible bully, drove that wretched first wife of his to an early grave. Mind you, Edith Procter was a poor sort of creature who never stood up for herself. Her sister Maud used to tell me some dreadful things." She lowered her voice "Violence and goodness knows what else!"

"Why didn't she leave him?"

Mrs Dudley looked at me pityingly. "Wives stuck with their husbands in those days," she said. "It was their duty."

"Poor June," I said, "it must have been awful for her."

"She did try to stand up for her mother," Mrs Dudley said, "but, of course, she was only a girl then. But when Edith died and he married again it was even worse. Leonard Hardy always wanted a son, someone to hand the business on to. So when Geraldine Miller got hold of him and married him, and when she had this boy, Malcolm, then June's nose was quite out of joint."

"But she got out, didn't she. She went to Bristol and trained as a nurse."

"Yes," Mrs Dudley said disapprovingly. "That was very foolish of her. She should have stayed and stuck up for herself .As it was, she was virtually disinherited. When her father died she only got a few thousand – Geraldine Hardy saw to that. She was a most unpleasant woman, stupid too – I used to sit on the Hospital Committee with her and she was forever interrupting and contradicting. She kept that son of hers tied to her apron strings until the day she died – some sort of kidney trouble I believe – so no wonder he went really wild after her death; spending money like water; a series of unsuitable attachments – most unsatisfactory."

She placed her knife and fork neatly in the centre of her plate and rang the little handbell she used to summon Elsie.

"Really," she said as Elsie brought in a perfect

lemon soufflé. "One could hardly blame June Hardy for getting rid of her half-brother." She spooned a generous portion of the pudding onto her plate and poured on some cream. "Now Sheila, take plenty – are you eating properly now you're on your own? You're starting to look quite haggard."

As I drove home I thought about what Mrs Dudley had said. At first I dismissed it out of hand, but the more I considered it the more I began to wonder if Mrs Dudley might be right. True, they were the last two people I would have ever considered as a couple, but they were of an age and had known each other for some time, and adversity and circumstance often draw the most unlikely people together. But whilst I could just about envisage them brought together in friendship, or even something stronger, I really couldn't believe that they would be capable of murder. Well, certainly not Ben Turner – but perhaps, just possibly, June. She was a strong-minded woman and if she was labouring under a sense of injustice at being cut out of her father's will, then she might, I suppose, have been tempted to do something about it.

"Well," said Rosemary, "how did it go with Mother?"

"She said I looked haggard."

"Oh dear, she will keep on saying things like that – thank goodness it was you!"

"No, it was fine, it meant I was positively encouraged to have a second helping of Elsie's gorgeous lemon souffle."

"Oh, I know, doesn't she do them well – and they come out like that every single time! Anything else?"

"She thinks that June Hardy and Ben Turner are having an affair and that June played Lady Macbeth to Ben's Macbeth and got him to murder Malcolm Hardy!"

"Oh for goodness sake!"

"Yes, well, I suppose it's possible. It would give Ben another reason for getting rid of Malcolm apart from having got the sack."

"But, honestly, can you *see* Ben doing something like that?"

"No, you're probably right..."

Rosemary pushed the plate of bourbons towards me. "Here, have another biscuit – stop you looking so haggard! No, actually, the thing I was going to tell you – you know, the thing I couldn't talk about when you rang – that was about the murder. Well, not the murder itself, but something that might have something to do with it."

"Really?"

"It's all very confidential – something I overheard Jack saying on the phone."

"I won't breathe a word."

"I only heard his side of the conversation of course so I *may* have got it all wrong, but it was to do with Diana's accounts at the practice. You know that Jack's firm does the audit? Well, because of Malcolm Hardy dying suddenly like that someone had to go and look at the books straight away. It sounds as though Diana hadn't expected that and so they found some sort of discrepancy – quite a large sum of money missing. Apparently she'd borrowed it to help her husband (you know he's got that small engineering firm) who's had a cash flow problem or whatever it is they call it. She was going to put it back when he'd got his new bank loan, it was only temporary, but still..."

"You mean if Malcolm Hardy had found out he might have made things very difficult for her?"

"Well, you know what sort of person he was – he'd have been awful!"

"Poor Diana. Still," I said absently biting into another bourbon, "she wouldn't have wanted him dead if that meant Jack's firm would go through the books and it would all come out."

"Unless," Rosemary said, "he'd found out already – before he died, I mean – and was going to do something about it."

"Something?"

"Oh, I don't know – some sort of legal action perhaps."

"So Diana might have had a real motive for killing him, not just dislike."

"It looks like it."

"So that means that all three vets had good reasons for wanting Malcolm Hardy dead.

"All three?"

"Yes," I said. "Because of that wretched man, poor Keith had a couple of enquiries hanging over him." And I told her what Kathy had told me.

"Oh dear. Still, I can't see any of them killing anyone, can you? I mean, they're so good with all the animals."

I laughed. "Oh Rosemary, really!"

"Yes, well, I suppose it does sound a bit silly put like that, but you know what I mean."

"Yes I do and you're quite right. It's very difficult to think of Diana, Ben or Keith as a murderer. Still, *somebody* killed Malcolm Hardy and if it wasn't any of them, who could it have been?"

I happened to be passing the surgery a few days later and on an impulse I went in. Alison was in reception entering something on the computer. She looked up as I went to the counter.

"Oh hello, Mrs Malory, can you hang on for a second while I finish this?"

"Of course."

I picked up a leaflet from the counter and was studying it when a large black and white cat jumped up beside me and rubbed against my hand.

"Oh," I exclaimed, "you've still got Toby!"

Toby was a stray that someone had brought in after he'd been injured by a car. He only had three legs but was amazingly mobile. He had been very much part of the surgery, presiding over the counter with a lordly air and very popular with all the clients. But the last few times I'd been in I hadn't seen him.

"There now!" Alison clicked the final key with an air of triumph. "That's done. Sorry to have kept you waiting, but when I'm entering figures, if I stop in the middle I have to start all over again! Yes, Toby's back again."

"When I didn't see him I wondered what had happened."

"His Lordship didn't like him being here – said it was unprofessional and Toby would have to be put down. Well, Diana wasn't having that." She stroked Toby lovingly and he arched his back in pleasure. "Malcolm made a fuss about it, but he had other things on his mind so he didn't press the point and we kept Toby out of the way. Mind you, if Malcolm hadn't died then I think he might have found some way of getting rid of Toby."

Toby, aware that he was being discussed began to show off, batting with his paw at the things on the counter.

"Oh dear, he's always doing that!" Alison said, rescuing a couple of ballpoint pens that had rolled under the counter. "I'm forever picking things up that he's knocked down. You're a wicked boy, aren't you?" she said lovingly while Toby purred complacently.

"Now then, what can I do for you?"

"I need some of that stuff I had before for Tris's ears. I've got a nasty feeling he's got mites in them. Diana did recommend something the last time he had them but I can't remember the name."

"Oh, I know what you mean. I'll just go and get it for you – it's out the back."

Alison went off and I continued to make a fuss of Toby who jumped down off the counter (making a perfect landing) and wound round my legs. I was just about to bend down to stroke him when Julie appeared. She looked quite different from the last time I'd seen her, during her quarrel with Malcolm Hardy. Now she looked very subdued and not at all well.

"Can I help you?" she asked, and her voice was quiet and listless.

"No, it's fine – Alison's looking after me. She's just gone to get something from out the back."

"Oh, right." She wandered out again and after a while Alison came back.

"There you are. I'm sure it will do the trick – just follow the instructions on the label, and if you're still worried come and see Diana. Shall I put it on your account?"

"Yes please." I put the spray into my bag. "I just saw Julie. I hardly recognised her as the same girl."

"Yes, she's changed a lot."

"I thought she looked dreadful – quite ill. Was she very upset about Malcolm Hardy's death?"

"She's not very well actually – some sort of tummy bug. But no, I don't think she was upset at all. They'd quarrelled you know, and I think he'd have found a way of getting rid of her from the practice if he'd still been around. No, she's been much better these days, really helpful."

"That's nice. Well, I'd better be going. I'm so glad Toby's back – the place really wouldn't be the same without him."

I turned to go when a thought struck me.

"Is the insulin you use on the animals the sort that humans use?" I asked.

Alison seemed surprised but answered, "We use Insuvet or Caninsulin, which are purely for vetinary use, but basically yes, they're the same." She looked at me curiously. "Are you asking because of Malcolm?"

"I suppose I am. I just wondered."

"The police wanted to know that as well," Alison said. "I suppose that was one more reason for suspecting someone here killed him." Then she burst out, "Honestly, Mrs Malory, there's no way it could be anyone here – I just wish to goodness they'd get it sorted so that we can all get back to normal!"

Chapter Ten

"I've got the tickets for *Iolanthe* for the Friday," Thea said, deftly inserting a spoonful of Farex into Alice's open mouth, "and Michael says he'll baby-sit, so that's all right. We'll have something to eat at the theatre beforehand and make a real night of it!"

"Oh lovely. I'm really looking forward to it. *Iolanthe*'s almost my favourite Gilbert and Sullivan."

"What is your favourite?"

I laughed. "I don't know – it changes every time I see one!"

"I love them all – except *Yeoman of the Guard*, which I've never really cared for."

"I know, the sad ending, which is not what one really wants from G&S. Oh dear…"

Alice, having decided that we weren't taking enough notice of her, waved her small fists in the air and sent the bowl and its contents flying.

"Wicked girl," Thea said fondly and went to get a cloth from the sink, while Alice, having achieved her objective, gave a gurgling laugh.

"Will she be all right with Michael when we go out?" I asked.

"He's very good with her, actually – and she doesn't play him up nearly as much as she does me. Anyway, he's got a list of instructions a mile long!"

So we were both happily relaxed as we sat in the theatre restaurant in Taunton before the performance. Because it was a local amateur opera group there were quite a few people from Taviscombe that we knew, coming to support relatives or friends in the cast.

"The same old faces," I said. "I do believe I could make a list of who'll be here every time."

But, just before the lights went down in the auditorium, someone I hadn't expected to see slipped into a seat in the row in front of us. It was Ben Turner. Then the lights went down and the first echoing notes of the overture swept over me and I gave my attention to the stage.

It was a good production and the singers were excellent. After a while the notes of a flute heralded the entrance of Phyllis. In her shepherdess costume with the blonde curls of her wig tumbling about her shoulders Kathy looked marvellous. The stage make-up heightened and emphasised her natural prettiness, in real life slightly faded, but now vibrant and charming. As she sang she moved gracefully in a dance and I heard a sort of gasp from the row in front and in the light from the stage I saw Ben Turner's face. He was completely rapt. So *that* was Kathy's secret.

"None shall part us from each other,
One in life and death are we."

Kathy's voice was clear and true.

It all fell into place now – Kathy's distress when Ben was sacked, the fear that he might have to go away; the return of her good spirits after Malcolm's death when his position in the practice was secure. But also the anxieties that Anthea had noted, Kathy's withdrawal from her parents in case they guessed her secret, the burden of guilt she and Ben must both feel thinking of his wife in a nursing home and knowing that they could never let anyone know of their relationship. I scarcely heard the rest of the first Act, my thoughts squirreling around. I kept looking at Ben. Whenever Kathy was on stage he leaned forward eagerly, when she was absent he slumped back in his seat, shielding his face with his hand.

In a sort of daze I followed Thea out in the interval – somehow I couldn't tell anyone, even her, what I had discovered – and made small talk about the production while we queued for our drinks. I was glad to be back in the darkened auditorium (Ben Turner had remained in his seat) and tried to lose myself in the music.

The Fairy Queen, her splendid contralto voice soaring, was embarked on that song which miraculously combines exquisite music with comic lyrics and topical references. The hint, now, of a long-forgotten scandal and the unreasoning power of love:

"Oh Captain Shaw!
Type of true love kept under!
Could thy Brigade
With cold cascade
Quench my great love, I wonder!"

Sullivan's music carried the opera forward but when Strephon (I found it hard to think of him as Jerry, who almost got transferred to Canada) and Phyllis were singing their final duet I saw such an expression of misery on Ben Turner's face that I had to look away.

"If by chance we should be parted," Kathy sang

" Broken hearted I should die –"

When it was over and the encores had been sung and the curtain calls had been taken, I fiddled around with my coat and my handbag, making sure that Ben Turner had left first. I didn't want him to know that I had seen him. Even if he hadn't realised how much he had given away that evening, I felt I had seen something I had no right to see and I didn't want to have to face him with some banal remark.

"Wasn't it good!" Thea enthused as we were driving home, "and wasn't Kathy marvellous. She looked absolutely terrific. She ought to go blonde – that wig really suited her."

"I don't think blonde is Kathy's style," I said. "Not in real life anyway."

"No, I suppose not," Thea agreed regretfully. "It's a pity though, she looked stunning."

Although I was longing to do so, I didn't tell Thea about Kathy and Ben because she knew Ben's daughter and it might be embarrassing for her to know their secret. But, because she too was concerned about Kathy, I did talk to Rosemary about it.

"Good heavens," Rosemary said. "He's years older than she is; he's got a grown-up daughter."

"And a grandchild," I said. "But I think Kathy might well be happier with an older man. Anyway, he obviously adores her – it was written all over his face."

"It's a wonder no one at the practice has spotted it."

"I expect they're on their guard all the time there. Such a strain for them both, poor things. But last night – well, Kathy did look marvellous with that costume and the make-up and everything, and, of course, Ben had absolutely no idea anyone who knew them would be watching him. I felt quite guilty!"

"I can imagine," Rosemary said sympathetically. "But what a wretched business, with his wife in a nursing home. She's still quite young and people with

Alzheimers can go on for years. So what sort of future can they have?"

"No future," I said sadly, "just going on as they are, I suppose. It *is* a shame, they're both such nice people."

"Well," Rosemary said, "this knocks Mother's little theory on the head – you know, about Ben and June Hardy. What a pity I can't tell her."

"I'm only surprised she didn't know about Kathy. It's not very often that something like that escapes her. Anyway," I continued thoughtfully, "it puts June Hardy in the clear over Malcolm's murder. If she didn't have an accomplice she couldn't have killed him, even if she had been able to get into the surgery somehow without being seen – never a very likely theory, if you come to think of it. It's just that she was the one with the greatest motive. All that money!"

"Well, I'm glad about that. June's such a nice person."

"Still," I said, "it does mean that two other nice people might have had motives for killing that horrible young man."

"Who? Oh, you mean Kathy and Ben Turner. Surely not!"

"I'm not saying they did it, but they had a motive. Kathy was desperately unhappy about Ben having to leave and so was he. And they were both on the spot when it happened."

"Would that really be enough reason to kill him?"

"Depends on the strength of their feelings. I'd say his are pretty strong."

"But *Kathy* – such a quiet, old-fashioned sort of girl. You couldn't think that!"

"It shook me when I found that she was having an

123

affair with a married man," I said. "It seemed so out of character. Especially when I thought it was some trendy young man from the opera group."

"Trendy?"

"I happened to see a bottle of Giorgio aftershave in her bathroom cabinet and drew the wrong conclusion. But, of course, Kathy must have given it to Ben as a Christmas present or something and he couldn't keep it at home – I mean it's so *not* him. Oh dear, isn't that sad!"

"How did you *happen* to see it?" Rosemary asked. "No – don't tell me! And yes, it is sad. No wonder Kathy couldn't confide in Anthea. I mean, she's devoted to Kathy but she would be horrified if she knew what was going on."

"I know. I think Jim would be quite sympathetic. Kathy's always been his favourite. But I don't suppose she could tell him."

"Goodness no," Rosemary said. "Anthea would have it out of him like a shot! No, poor Kathy's got no one to confide in. Unless..."

"No," I said firmly. "I'm *not* getting involved."

"She really looks up to you..."

"No!"

"Oh well. I'll put the kettle on. Tea or coffee?"

"Incidentally," Rosemary said as she was warming the teapot, "you remember what I told you about Diana?"

"Yes."

"Well, it's all right. Apparently Jack had a word with Edward Drayton and he told June all about it – Diana borrowing the money, that is. Anyway, June was very understanding and, since Diana's paid back the money now, she isn't going to do anything about it."

"Oh, well done June."

"Like I said, she's a nice person. She said she obviously didn't approve of what Diana had done, but she understood why she did it and is prepared to say no more about it."

"That must be a relief all round. Of course!" I said so suddenly that Rosemary looked up from pouring the tea. "Of course, June told me on Sunday after church that she had to see Edward about something. That must have been what it was."

"The problem Diana has now," Rosemary said "is having to pay back to Malcolm Hardy's estate the money he put into the practice."

"Oh goodness, that will be difficult won't it? I mean, I knew she'd have to find someone to take over the partnership now that he's dead..." I broke off. "And this means that she couldn't have murdered Malcolm, even to stop him finding out about borrowing the money!"

"What on earth do you mean?"

"Don't you see? If he was dead she'd have to pay back his share. She certainly wouldn't have wanted *that*."

"No, I suppose not."

"It's going to be really hard for her now that he's dead."

"Oh, but the practice must be quite profitable. The surgery always seems to be full whenever I take one of the animals."

"I'm sure it is, but I think it was a very large sum of money Malcolm Hardy put in."

"Well," Rosemary said, "I expect all the legal things will take a while so perhaps something will turn up."

"I hope so. I like Diana – I'm glad she isn't a suspect any more."

"You never really thought she might be, did you?"

"I don't know. It must have been *someone* connected with the practice who killed him and there aren't that many people to choose from."

Rosemary poured some more water into the teapot and stirred it thoughtfully. "I still find it extraordinary that someone should have murdered him in that peculiar way. I mean, it might not have actually killed him, if they'd got the amount of insulin wrong and if whoever it was didn't know exactly what sort of tablets he was taking and what sort of effect they'd have on each other. If you think of it, it must surely have been someone who knew him pretty well."

"Perhaps," I suggested, "whoever it was didn't mean to *murder* him at all. Perhaps they just wanted to make him ill, or give him a fright or something."

"Who on earth would want to do that?"

"I don't know," I admitted, "but you must admit it's a possibility. A sort of gesture that went wrong?"

"That's too complicated for me," Rosemary said. "Anyway, let's talk about something a bit more cheerful. Did I tell you that Delia's going to be in the school play? They're doing 'Toad of Toad Hall' for Christmas and she's going to be one of the weasels. Jilly's going mad trying to make the costume!"

That evening I had a committee meeting that didn't finish until quite late. As I drove home along the road behind Kathy's flat I passed Ben Turner's old Land

Rover parked there. Somehow the fact that he'd had to park around the corner from the flat, with all that that implied, made me very sad. They were two nice people who were, when you came to think of it, doing no one any harm. Ben's wife was incapable of caring what he did now and yet, just *because* they were nice and didn't want to hurt anyone, they felt obliged to live in this hole and corner fashion. The fact remained that they were considering the feelings of Ben's daughter and Kathy's parents and, even if they were prepared to face it themselves, they didn't want their families put through the misery of the gossip and disapproval of a small town. It didn't seem fair.

It did occur to me, though, that if they were determined to keep their relationship secret, then if Malcolm Hardy had found out about them, one or both of them might have had a good reason for wanting to silence him. I tried to put this uncomfortable thought out of my mind and when I got home concentrated on placating the animals who hate me to go out in the evening, thereby depriving them of a lap to sit on or a piece of forbidden chocolate reluctantly disgorged. As I made myself a hot drink Foss weaved round my legs, giving me a tiny nip to declare his presence, while Tris sat with his head on one side fixing me with a mesmeric stare of immense reproach.

"Oh all right," I said, giving in as I always did. "I'll give you something *now*."

I put a handful of cat and dog biscuits on the tray with my drink and, with the two of them hard on my heels, I went into the sitting-room, pacified them with treats and put on the television.

I seemed to have switched on half way through a

drama set, as far as I could see, (it was all very dark and, to help the atmosphere, raining heavily) in some Northern town. I picked up the remote control to switch it off, since it was decidedly not the sort of entertainment I was looking for at the end of a tiring day, when my attention was caught by the dialogue.

The woman, who was about Kathy's age, was protesting to the man I took to be her lover.

"It's no good," she said. "We'll be hurting too many people if we go on with this."

She looked a bit like Kathy too, though the man was much younger than Ben and better looking.

"But don't you see...?" he said.

"No, Mal," she interrupted, "it's impossible and you know it!"

There was one of those pauses when you know the character is winding himself up to make some powerful speech. Then he burst out,

"Kathy, we love each other, you know that! There's no way we can ignore it, it won't go away just because we pretend it doesn't exist." The coincidence of her name being the same kept me riveted. "All right, Janice is my wife but we've been living as strangers for years now. We don't communicate any more – perhaps we never did. And now this fabulous chance has come along for us to be together forever. How can we let it slip?"

The woman (who distracted me by an irritating habit of tucking stray locks of hair behind her ears) considered this.

"It's wrong," she said at last. "How could we do such a thing!"

"It would be wrong," he declared, "not to do it. It's

our one chance of happiness, surely we deserve that? In your heart you know I'm right. Be brave, Kathy, and face the truth!"

"Oh Mal! Yes! You're right. Of course I'll come with you!"

There was the obligatory embrace as the credits rolled and I was left wondering what the fabulous chance was that would let them be together forever, and wishing that such a chance could occur for my Kathy. But, of course, whatever the chance, and however fabulous, she would never take it. People like Kathy and Ben didn't do things like that, nor, probably, would any of the people I knew in Taviscombe.

Chapter Eleven

There is nothing so profoundly irritating and frustrating as having something happen to one's computer. Especially if, like me, you haven't the remotest idea how the thing works or what to do to make things better. You daren't experiment in case you do something irretrievably awful to the mysterious and omnipotent entity called The Hard Drive, so you are left with a feeling of helplessness and rage. In my innocence, as a novice, I had assumed that once I'd grasped the basic principles (I really only used the thing as a sort of super typewriter) all would be plain sailing. How wrong I was. The wretched thing kept freezing (I believe that's the proper term) and I could only switch it off, getting that horrid, patronising notice that told me I'd exited incorrectly and not to do it again. After this had happened a couple of times, I left it to itself, hoping that by some miracle it would be all right the next day. And the next day. But, of course, it wasn't, so eventually I had to phone Michael.

"Lord! I don't know. It could be anything!"

"Oh, for goodness sake," I said impatiently, "you must have some idea!"

"Computers are funny things," he said maddeningly. "It could be anything."

"I know *that*. Can you come and look at it?"

"Honestly Ma, I don't think I'd be able to do any good. What you should do is take it to my friend Dave, he's an absolute whizz at fixing them. Just give him a ring, I'm sure he can help. You'll only have to take the tower so I'll come round and disconnect all the wires and things."

Michael's friend Dave, who I remembered as charming but eccentric, seemed willing to help and gave me directions for reaching him. It was a pleasant day and I quite enjoyed the drive to Hoccombe St Mary's until I reached the narrow lane that I was required to take to get to the cottage. It was, in fact, a very narrow lane with virtually no passing places and I peered anxiously ahead, praying that I wouldn't meet another car. I had gone for about a mile when I went round a bend (fortunately very slowly) and found myself nose to nose with a large estate car. I sat for a moment, hoping that the other person (obviously a local from the speed the car was travelling) would back, but as I looked again I saw that the driver was Claudia Drummond and, from the way she sat there impatiently tapping her fingers on the steering wheel, she had no intention of moving.

I hate reversing, especially in our lanes where large stones in the hedges, hidden by the lush foliage, are a constant threat to one's paintwork. Anyway, now I have a bit of arthritis in my neck the whole exercise is quite painful. With bad grace I started to reverse, lurching a bit from side to side of the narrow lane and having to stop and correct myself. Eventually, after what seemed ages, I found a gateway and eased my car into it. The estate car swept past, and I noticed with fury that Claudia Drummond didn't even raise her hand in token thanks for my manoeuvre.

Still shaken by anger at the encounter I went on and finally found the cottage. I couldn't make anyone hear at the front door so I went round the back and found

Dave in what I took to be his workshop. He greeted me cheerfully and, fetching my computer from the car, invited me in.

It was, actually, difficult to *get* in, since most of the available floor space was taken up by benches with a variety of computers, monitors, keyboards and boxes of what I took to be spare parts. There were also ancient filing cabinets, old swivel chairs and desks, what seemed to be the detritus of many abandoned offices. Dave dusted off one of the swivel chairs and I sat down in it gingerly. He plugged my computer in and questioned me patiently about the problem. After a bit he said, "I think you need more memory – I can do that for you, no problem."

"That's marvellous," I said.

"Well, leave it with me and I'll try that and see how it goes."

"Right, I'll do that then. Thanks very much."

I got up to go and Dave said, "It's not very easy to reverse from here – not a lot of space. You'll do better to go up the lane to the fork in the road by the big house and turn there. That's what most people do."

"The big house?"

"Yes, Hoccombe Court."

"Is that where the Drummonds live?" I asked.

"That's right."

I told him about my experience with Claudia Drummond and he gave a short laugh.

"Typical! Dreadful woman! Very unpopular in the village."

"I can imagine."

"When they first came here she tried to run everything and when people wouldn't stand for that she decided we were a lot of ignorant clod-hoppers and found other things to amuse herself with."

"Really?"

"Oh yes. I imagine she thinks she's being discreet, but you know what it's like in the country, *someone* is always around. There's quite a lot of gossip."

"Gossip about what?"

"Young men mostly. Some of the hunting set – she's very into all that – and there've been a couple of others. One was a schoolmaster, I think, and I don't know who the most recent is – or perhaps she's tired of him already because he hasn't been around lately."

"You seem very well informed about their movements," I said.

"Well, the cottage is almost on the road here so I can see who goes by. There's not a lot of traffic along here, mostly for me or for the big house. Living alone you take more notice, I suppose, of people going by."

"But what about Sir Robert ?"

"He's away a lot. He works in Bristol and then he's off on these conferences they all seem to go to."

"But surely he *must* know what's going on?"

"Oh, he knows sure enough, but he must have known what he was taking on when he married her – she led a racketty sort of life before then, from what I can gather – and she's a good bit younger than him. No, I reckon he thinks that if he pretends nothing's happening then it's all right and people will take things at their face value."

"It seems an odd sort of relationship."

"I think he's the kind of man who really only cares about his work – they say he's very ambitious – and he wanted someone who'd look good at functions and what have you and give him a bit of prestige. She's certainly a handsome woman."

"I suppose so." I picked up my bag and started to thread my way through the various objects to the door. "Oh, by the way, what did the latest young man look like?" I asked.

Dave seemed surprised at my question, but he said, "Tall, dark hair, drives a grey Range Rover."

"Malcolm Hardy!" I exclaimed. "I thought so."

"Someone you know?"

"I don't know him exactly – but he was the vet – the one who was killed. That's why you haven't seen him around here lately."

"Good heavens! I read about that in the local rag. I don't think there was a photo so I never made the connection."

I thought for a minute then said, "I don't suppose you can remember the last time he came here, can you?"

"As a matter of fact I can. It was the day I had a delivery of some monitors and they were the wrong sort so I had to make a heck of a lot of phone calls to sort it out. Hang on a minute, I can find the exact date if you like."

He went over to a sort of wall planner that was sellotaped to one of the filing cabinets and studied it.

"Yes, here we are. Look," he pointed to a scribbled entry in one of the squares, "it was the twenty-fifth."

I bent over to look and exclaimed, "Good heavens! That was the day he died!"

"Really?"

"What time was he here?"

Dave thought for a moment. "Lunchtime. It must

have been lunchtime when he went down, just after twelve. I remember thinking it was no use ringing the wholesalers because everyone would be on their lunch break."

"And did you hear him going back up the lane?" I asked tentatively.

"I certainly did. He was going like a bat out of hell. I just hoped he didn't meet anyone because there'd have been a bad accident if he had."

He paused and said curiously, "Forgive me asking, but why do you want to know all this?"

"Well, you see, the people at the surgery said Malcolm Hardy had been out at lunchtime, a few hours before he died, but no one knew where he'd been. I think the police will be very grateful to hear about all this. Look, I know Inspector Eliot (he's my god-daughter's husband), so I'll tell him what you've told me and I expect he'll want you to make a statement. Is that all right? I know it's very valuable information."

"Sure, I don't mind." He looked at me sharply. "Do you think Claudia Drummond had something to do with this chap's death?"

"I honestly don't know. But I'm sure it's really important to know where he spent those last few hours." I paused for a moment. "The police will want to talk to her. Will that make things awkward for you? I'm sure they won't let her know that it was you who told them about Malcolm Hardy's visit."

"No skin off my nose if they do. We're not exactly on calling terms!"

"Well," I said, moving cautiously towards the door, "thanks for everything."

"I'll let you know when this is ready," he said,

tapping my computer. "Shouldn't be more than a couple of days – depends how soon the bits come through. Don't forget – go up to the fork and turn."

I walked back through the garden, admiring a splendid rhus in its colourful glory, and got back into the car. I drove very slowly up to the fork in the lane and turned the car. Then, making sure that there was no one about, I got out and went over to look at Hoccombe Court, or at least what I could see of it. Although it was at the end of a short drive lined with shrubs and small trees, it stood on a slight eminence and so was fairly visible from the road. It was a handsome small manor house, typical of those in this part of the county, built of mellow brick with some half-timbering, bleached with age. There didn't seem to be anyone about so perhaps there were no live-in servants, which would have made Claudia's little escapades easier to manage. The garden was well-tended; the grass cut and the shrubs neatly trimmed, signs of professional attention, probably some landscape specialist rather than an old-fashioned gardener, since it gave the impression that competence rather than love had dictated the layout and planting. I stood for a moment gazing abstractedly at the scene, then I got back into the car and went home.

That evening I phoned Roger. Jilly answered the phone and we chatted a bit about the children, then I said, "Do you think I could have a word with Roger?"

"Of course. He's reading Alex his third bedtime story so expect he'll be glad to be released!"

"Roger," I said, when he came to the phone. "I'm so sorry to bother you at home, but I found out today something I think you ought to know."

I told him what I had gathered from Dave and he said, "Well done Sheila! I always knew that the Taviscombe MI5 was our best source of information."

"Very funny! But seriously, Malcolm Hardy was obviously having some sort of affair with Claudia Drummond. Rosemary and I saw them together one day up by Brendon Two-Gates."

"You see! Nowhere is safe from the perfect spy system."

"*And*," I went on, "it looks as if there might have been a quarrel between them that lunchtime. I mean, Dave said Malcolm drove off in a fury and all the girls at the surgery remarked on how bad tempered he was when he got back. *Something* must have happened."

"Could be."

"Actually, if you think about it, it's quite possible that he took, or was given, the insulin there, at Claudia's. So no one at the surgery need have been involved at all!"

"I'd need to get medical advice about the reaction time of the insulin."

"But it's possible?"

"It might be."

"So will you go and see Claudia Drummond?"

"In view of what you've told me, yes, of course."

"Roger," I said hesitantly, "if you do go and see her, you won't let her know that Dave told me about Malcolm going there, will you?"

He laughed. "Surely you know that we never disclose our sources of information."

"Yes, well. And Roger – you will let me know what you find out, won't you?"

I didn't really expect to hear from Roger immediately. Adopting the mock severe tone he does on these occasions, he'd said that it would be confidential information, which of course couldn't be divulged, but I was fairly sure he'd at least give me a hint about what he found out. In any case I was pretty much involved in a gardening project that was taking up most of my time and energy. Reg Parry, who does most of the heavy work in my garden, had finally, grumbling every step of the way, ("Thic deuritzia she's a fine bush – tid'n no sense to move 'er") dug up several shrubs that had been cluttering up the main herbaceous border for years so I was taking the opportunity to replan the whole bed. The house was littered with bits of paper with rough pencil sketches, and kind Thea had made me several plans on her computer with the various options marked out.

"You know," I said to Thea when she brought them round, "I think it might be a good idea to go to a garden centre and see what's actually on offer."

"You could order things from catalogues," Thea said sensibly.

"I know, but I do like to *see* the plants. I always expect too much of pictures in catalogues. Actually there's this splendid new place that opened the other side of Kilve. They say it's really good – they've got lots of unusual things."

"Is unusual a good idea?" Thea asked cautiously. "They might not be suitable."

"Oh well, I'll probably stick to the old faithfuls, with just a *few* experiments." I picked up one of the designs she had made. "I must say I like this one. I've always wanted *drifts* of things, and I love the way the plants spread out over the path at this end."

I took Thea's plan with me, when I made my expedition to the new garden centre, as well as numerous lists I had made. But, of course, once I was confronted by the richness and variety of all the plants on offer, I rather lost my head and soon my large trolley was full of things that I felt in my heart Thea would call unsuitable. I was just considering my potential purchases when a voice behind me said,

"Sheila! Sheila Malory! What a surprise – I haven't seen you for ages. How are you?"

My heart sank. Beryl Morton is an old acquaintance, but one I try to avoid whenever possible since she is the most terrible bore. Trapped as I was by a heavily ladened trolley there was no escape, so I greeted her with what I hope passed for enthusiasm.

"Beryl! How nice to see you. How are you?"

That was a mistake since she spent a good ten minutes telling me about the bad bout of enteritis she'd just recovered from, which led on to her son's tendonitis and her husband's cartilage operation. My eyes were glazing over as I leaned for support on the handles of my trolley, when I suddenly heard a name I knew.

"He had the operation done privately of course, in Bristol. Sir Robert Drummond did it – he's very eminent in his field you know."

"Yes," I said, suddenly alert and eager to hear more. "So I've heard."

"Actually, Desmond knows him slightly, that's why he was very anxious that Sir Robert should do it."

"Really?"

"Such a nice man. I believe he's due to retire soon, though he's very active for his age and, of course, he does have that wretched diabetes to content with – though I suppose that's nothing nowadays is it, not with all the new drugs and injections and things."

"No, I suppose not. How interesting that it should have been Sir Robert – I ran into his wife quite recently."

I reflected that the white lie was almost justified since she had almost run into me!

"Oh did you? What did you make of her? She's his second wife, of course."

"I didn't really take to her," I said truthfully.

"No, well, I believe she isn't generally liked."

"How did they meet?" I asked. "I mean, she's so much younger than him."

"She was a nurse – South African, of some sort. I think that was when he was working in Durban. Which reminds me, did I tell you that Desmond's sister Janet is going to buy a house in Spain? We all think it's a great mistake, well, you know how difficult property abroad can be..."

She went on, without apparently drawing breath, for some time, until I finally managed to break in and make some excuse to get away.

When I got home and unloaded the plants I found that I'd forgotten to get the delphiniums which were to form an integral part of the border.

"Never mind," I said to Foss, who was investigating a pot of Japanese anemones by scooping out the earth with his paw, "we now know that Robert Drummond is a diabetic, so that there must be a supply of insulin readily to hand, and that Claudia Drummond used to be a nurse, so would know exactly what would happen if Malcolm Hardy was given insulin on top of the drugs he was already taking. I think," I said, " I'd better let Roger know before he has a word with her."

I moved indoors to the phone leaving Foss, who had abandoned the flower pot and was putting in some serious digging of his own in the newly dug border.

Chapter Twelve

"At first she denied the whole thing," Roger said. "Insisted Malcolm Hardy was a mere acquaintance and said he'd never been near the place that day. But when I told her we had a witness who'd seen him, she came over all pathetic – said her husband was so jealous, and so on and so forth."

We were sitting in my kitchen with cups of coffee and a plate of chocolate digestive biscuits (Roger's favourites) while he brought me up to date on his interview with Claudia Drummond.

"That's not what I heard," I said. "Mind you, he may have reached the limits of his patience. Perhaps he'd threatened to divorce her – I'm sure she wouldn't like that."

"I certainly got the impression that she doesn't want him to hear about this particular episode."

"Did you get any idea *why* Malcolm Hardy went there? I mean, I wouldn't have thought they'd risk being together at her place, especially since he's got a large house of his own with no encumbrances. A much more convenient place to meet, wouldn't you think?"

"I gather he suddenly turned up to have it out with her, or at least that's what she said."

"Have what out?"

"He wanted her to leave her husband and go and live with him."

"Fat chance! So what did she say about that?"

"Oh, how she'd never looked on it as a serious affair, how she'd never leave her husband – that sort of thing."

"And how," I enquired, "did he take all of that?"

"Badly. She didn't go into details but it sounds as if he was furious – I suppose he thought she'd led him on. She said she was afraid of him, thought he might get violent."

"I can't see Claudia Drummond being afraid of anyone in that way! But I suppose she might have been afraid that he'd tell her husband, and, like I said, it might have been the last straw for him."

"Possibly." Roger took another biscuit and bit into it thoughtfully.

"So," I went on, "she might very well have had a reason for getting rid of him. And, as I told you, there's insulin in the house. She could have put something in his drink."

"Ah – that's the point."

"What?"

"He didn't have anything to drink there."

"That's what she said? "

"Yes."

"And you believed her?"

"Yes, I think I do. From what she told me, it was a real stand-up row and then he stormed out. Not a situation when he might have downed a peaceful whisky!"

"You don't think she might have tried to smooth him down, given him a drink to calm him?"

"Not really. Anyway, your friend Dave said that he drove off down the lane in a tearing hurry – just like a man who'd had a row, in fact."

"Yes," I said regretfully, "I suppose that's true. And he was certainly still in a dreadful temper when he got back to the surgery. But if all that's so, then where did he get the alcohol that was found in his blood?"

"I can only imagine he stopped off somewhere on the way back to have a quick drink. I expect he felt the need for one by then!"

"I suppose so."

"Which means," Roger sighed, "checking every pub between Hoccombe St Mary and Taviscombe!"

"Oh dear. Here," I pushed the plate towards him, "have the last biscuit to keep your strength up!"

"So I'm afraid," I said regretfully to Rosemary when she rang me that evening, "it looks as if Claudia didn't murder him after all. I mean, if he didn't drink anything while he was there. And he's not likely to have stood still while she pumped him full of insulin!"

"Pity," Rosemary said, "she was my favourite suspect. Dreadful woman! Oh well, I expect Roger will sort it out eventually. Now, what I wanted to ask you is can you come to Taunton with me next Tuesday morning? I thought I'd start my Christmas shopping *really* early this year."

"Oh bother, no I can't manage Tuesday. I foolishly let Anthea persuade me to help her serve the coffee at the flu clinic. You know how she won't take no for an answer!"

"Oh, poor you! Never mind, we could make it Thursday if you like."

"Thursday would be lovely," I said gratefully. "It will be something to look forward to."

The flu clinic, where the over-65s are given their flu jabs, takes place in one of the many church halls with which Taviscombe abounds. It's very well run and is really quite a social occasion because the patients are required to sit down for 10 minutes after they've been injected to make sure there are no ill effects, and to keep them there they're offered coffee and bicuits. After which, of course, they sit chatting and the problem is to get them moved on so that the next batch can be processed.

The thing was supposed to start at ten o'clock but when I arrived there was already a queue waiting to get in – the over-65s being of that generation who always, conscientiously, arrive early for everything. The hall had been set up with rows of chairs and screened-off tables with the medical equipment and I saw Anthea waving at me from the counter at the far end of the hall where the kitchen was.

"I've got the kettles on," she said, before I'd even got my coat off. "There's no urn, unfortunately, but I think we can manage if we keep the kettles going. Can you put the biscuits out – they're in that tin over there."

Silently giving thanks for the absence of an urn (urns and I are not compatible), I put some biscuits onto the plates and set out the cups and saucers and bowls of sugar.

"There'll be quite a rush once they get going," Anthea said, "so can you put some coffee into the cups all ready? About a heaped teaspoonful should be about right, most old people like it a bit weak. Oh, and can you open a carton of milk and pour it into one of those big jugs then I can get at it more easily."

It is generally recognised by those of us who engage in good works with her that Anthea will always take command and so most of us meekly do her bidding – though Vera Parrish (a born rebel) was once heard to mutter under her breath, "What did your last slave die of?"

The expected rush began and I was soon too busy to do more than spoon coffee into cups, gather up the used ones and replenish the plates of biscuits. After a while I also found myself at the sink washing up and it was while I was doing this that June Hardy suddenly appeared.

"Hello Sheila," she said. "If I could just have a word?"

"Of course."

"It's about the Red Cross auction sale. You know, of course, that I shall have to dispose of the house now that Malcolm's dead."

"Yes, I suppose so..."

"Well, the larger pieces of furniture will have to go to the sale-room, but I thought perhaps some of the smaller pieces and the ornaments and so forth, might go to the auction. They should raise quite a good sum for the Red Cross."

"Are you sure?"

"Oh yes, there's nothing there that has any significance for me – I shall be glad to think that the things might do some good."

"It's very generous of you," I said.

"Not really – selfish if anything. It'll save me having to deal with a lot of it. Martin Preston has said he'll have the stuff collected and taken along to the Red Cross depot so that's no problem. No, what I'd like you to do is put stickers on anything you think might sell."

"Stickers are no use!" Anthea had come up behind us.

"Really?" June said.

"No – either they fall off or they leave dreadful

sticky patches when you remove them. What you want are tie-on labels."

"Oh."

"I've got a box of them at home – I used them when Mother died and we had to separate out who was going to have what in the family."

"Perhaps," June suggested, "you could give Sheila a hand then."

Since this was patently what Anthea had had in mind (she loves poking about in other people's houses – but then, don't we all?) she agreed enthusiastically.

"Well that's very kind of you both," June said. "I've got the keys from the solicitors now so if you'd like to call in at the Larches on your way there I can let you have them. Now I must go and collect my old people – I'm sure they must have finished their coffee by now. Oh yes, there's Mrs Benedict wandering off. I'd better go and catch her before she goes out the door – not exactly Altzheimers, but she's very vague. Let me know which day will suit you."

The Hardy house (I'd forgotten it had a name – it was called Willowbank, though there wasn't a willow in sight), had that damp musty smell when we went in that you get in houses that have been shut up for a while. It was a very long time since I'd been inside; it must have been over twenty years ago, when old Mr Hardy was alive and my mother and I sometimes went to tea there. I'd also forgotten just how big it was, a real Edwardian family house, three storeys high and with attics and cellars and all sorts of out-buildings whose original use was now lost in the mists of time.

"The central heating's still on," Anthea said, putting her hand on one of the large, old fashioned radiators, "but it feels dreadfully damp – everything's going to be covered in mould!"

I shivered slightly. "It's a bit creepy," I said.

"Nonsense," Anthea said briskly. "It's just that the stained glass in the door and windows makes it seem so dark."

She switched on the electric light and we looked around us.

The ochre and black encaustic tiles on the floor, and the dark green painted lincrusta which gave way to sage green paper on the walls, certainly did little to lighten the spacious hall with its heavy oak staircase carpeted in crimson. There was a large grandfather clock and a massive carved oak chest against one wall and dark, indeterminate oil paintings in heavy gilt frames hung on the other. The drawing room was equally of its period, with long amber velvet curtains, vast chairs and sofas, which looked as if they could accommodate a race of giants, and a plethora of small occasional tables loaded with "objects".

"Good heavens above!" Anthea exclaimed. "No wonder June doesn't want to keep any of this!"

"It looks just like it did when we used to visit all those years ago," I said. "It's quite extraordinary. How could a young man like Malcolm live in such surroundings?"

"Mind you," Anthea went on, examining a pair of elaborate pewter candlesticks on the piano, "it's all very good quality. You don't get workmanship like this nowadays."

"Actually," I said, looking around me, "some of this

stuff really ought to go to Sothebys or somewhere –
those miniatures, for example, those silver snuff boxes
and that French clock on the mantelpiece. They'd
never realise their proper value in a Red Cross sale
here at Taviscombe."

"But June did say..." Anthea began.

"Yes, I know," I said, "and if she wants to she can
always give the money they raise to the Red Cross or
some other worthy cause."

"Yes, I suppose so."

Anthea was moving out of the drawing room back
into the hall and into the room beyond.

"Good gracious!" I heard her exclaim and I went to
join her in what used to be the dining room.

The contrast was certainly startling. This, presumably, was where Malcolm Hardy had actually lived.
There were no rich velvet curtains here; instead there
were fancy slatted blinds. Instead of elaborate chande-
liers there were a multiplicity of spotlights in chrome
holders and instead of the heavy furniture there were
chairs and tables of twisted chrome and smoked glass.
The walls had been covered in a sort of coarse cream
linen and were hung with abstract "modern" paintings. The whole thing looked like a Style page from
one of the Sunday supplements.

"Whatever would his father have said!" Anthea
demanded.

There seemed to be no answer to that so I continued to look about me. There was what I believe is
called a Work Station at one end of the room, with a
very elaborate-looking computer and next to it a
large television, video and CD player, all in one.
Beyond that was a glass and chrome trolley which

held a number of bottles, ice buckets and general drinking paraphenalia.

Anthea, following my gaze, stared disapprovingly.

"All that drink," she said. "He must have been an alcoholic!"

I moved over and examined the bottles more closely. There were three different kinds of gin, half a dozen single malt whiskies, and various kinds of rum and vodka that I'd never even heard of.

"I think they're as much for show," I said, "as for drinking."

Anthea gave me a sharp look and went out of the room. I heard her going upstairs and went back into the hall. The wide hall turned into a narrow passage-way leading to the kitchen. Just before the kitchen there were two doors on either side of the passage. I tried the first, that appeared to lead out into the drive, but it was locked. The other opened into a large walk-in larder of a kind that you don't see very often nowadays. There were wide shelves and marble slabs and it was well-lit with a large window at one end. The shelves were empty except for a few heavy earthernware jars and a great shallow dish of a kind I remember from my childhood that we used to "put down" eggs in isinglass for the winter. I went over to the window, which looked out onto the garden. One of the sash-cords was broken and hung down, stirring occasionally in the draught from the ill-fitting window. I shivered slightly, turned and went out and into the kitchen. Although it hadn't been modernised and still had a large dresser with shelves displaying plates and dishes, and a large scrubbed wooden table with a couple of chairs, there was a modern sink unit, a big refrigerator and a nice new cooker. But the cooker was suspiciously clean and it seemed probable that Malcolm Hardy, when he cooked for himself, had used the large, shiny microwave that stood on a table by the window.

I had just opened the refrigerator (empty except for a few cans of beer – but presumably June had got rid of any perishable stuff) when I heard Anthea calling from upstairs. Rather guiltily I slammed the door shut and went to join her. I found her outside one of the bedrooms.

"Just look at that!" she said flinging the door open wider.

Just as he had modernised one of the rooms downstairs so he had completely altered the room he had used as his bedroom. There were the same blinds at the windows and the same linen paper on the walls. Not that much of the walls were visible, although it was a fair sized room.

They were all covered with works of art. And, indeed, they *were* works of art, reproductions of paintings and drawings by Botticelli, Cranach, Velasquez, Ingres, Degas, Bonnard, Picasso and many others – a comprehensive history of art, you might say, and all with one theme: they all portrayed the naked female form.

"Just look at that!" Anthea repeated.

"Good gracious," I said.

Anthea seemed to find that an inadequate response.

"I think it's absolutely disgusting. What poor June must have thought when she saw it..."

I went further into the room. Apart from a fitted cupboard the only things in the room were a king-size bed with a sort of fur coverlet over it and a very large television set. I'm afraid I can never quite resist teasing Anthea a little.

"I believe it's what's called a bachelor pad," I said. "Very stylish and modern."

"Disgraceful – just like all that dreadful rubbish you get on television."

The bathroom had also been modernised but the other bedrooms had been left in their old-fashioned splendour. I indicated the stairs leading up to the third floor.

"I think it's just attics up here," I said. "Shall we go up?"

Anthea shook her head. "No," she said. "I'm going to make a start downstairs – you go ahead though and let me know if there's anything suitable up there. I really don't know *what* we're going to do about labelling things for the auction."

The rooms on the top floor were small and all had sloping ceilings; presumably the servants' rooms way back in the early 1900s when the house was first built. Now they were filled with boxes and tea chests all dusty and forgotten, with the odd object – a glass vase or broken china ornament – left abandoned on the narrow mantelpieces. I lifted some old newspapers from one of the boxes and found a jumbled collection of books, framed photographs (mostly faded with age), odd pieces of china and the usual collection of coathangers that always seem to find their way into any collection of discarded objects. The thought of sifting through this detritus of a bygone age, which at other times might have appealed to me, suddenly seemed too much. It made me feel melancholy and depressed, so I quickly made my way downstairs to the comfort of Anthea's bracing presence in the kitchen.

Chapter Thirteen

As most people would agree, there is nothing quite so irritating as a dripping tap, and if you are a middle-aged female living alone it's really difficult to find someone to do that sort of small job any more. Fortunately Michael is good at that kind of thing and said he'd come round after work and fix it for me.

"There you are," he said, coming downstairs from the bathroom, "all done. It just needed a new washer."

"Bless you. Will you have a cup of tea or something stronger?"

"Tea will be fine. Have you got any of that chocolate cake left?"

I got out the cups and the cake and while we were waiting for the kettle to boil Michael said, "You'll never believe what's happened."

"What?" I asked anxiously. "Something to do with Thea or Alice?"

"No, no, nothing to do with us. It's about the Malcolm Hardy affair you seem to be taking such an interest in."

"Oh, really?"

"It turns out that June Hardy might not inherit the estate after all."

"What! But I thought..."

"So did everyone. He had no direct heir, so she inherits. *But* it turns out that he may well have an heir."

"I don't understand."

"That girl Julie, his girlfriend, she's going to have a baby and she says it's his."

"Good heavens!"

I poured the water into the teapot and asked, "Why did no one know before?"

"It's a bit complicated. Apparently Malcolm Hardy was furious when she told him and wanted her to get rid of it."

"Poor girl!"

"Well, she wouldn't and that's what they split up over – well that and the fact that he wanted her out of his life anyway because he'd just started an affair with someone else."

"Claudia Drummond."

Michael laughed. "I might have guessed *you*'d have known about that! Well, anyway, things were pretty difficult between them when he died. Then afterwards she didn't know what to do. She was living with her parents and she hadn't told them."

"No, from what I know Cynthia Barnes isn't the sort of person you could confide in, even if you were her daughter, and I did hear that her husband is a very difficult man."

"That's more or less what we gathered. This Julie girl was afraid to tell her parents, but obviously it wasn't something she could keep hidden forever, and they found out. Actually, it was the father who approached us, as Malcolm Hardy's solicitors, to see if there was any chance of getting money from the estate – money does seem to be his main consideration; just what he can get out of it, no real feeling for his daughter."

"Did you tell him about old Mr Hardy's will?"

"No. Too early to say anything, the baby hasn't been born yet. I mean..."

"Yes I see..."

"And even when it has been born they have to prove that it was Malcolm Hardy's."

"Can they do that now he's dead, from DNA and so forth?"

"Yes. It'll be a complicated business, but they can do it. But even if the child *is* his direct heir, we'll have to set up some sort of trust fund. It's by no means cut and dried, and we certainly can't go handing out money at this stage."

"Poor June," I said. "Though perhaps she won't mind too much if she doesn't inherit – she's always seemed to be the sort of person who doesn't care too much about money. The only thing she really *does* care about now is her work. I know she loves being at The Larches, she's done a wonderful job there."

"Well it's early days yet. Is there another cup in the pot? Then I must be off if I'm going to be in time for Alice's bath."

The weekend was wet and windy but whatever the weather Tris always insists on his walk so, when the rain had more or less eased off into a thin drizzle, I put on a raincoat and the hideous waterproof hat that I only wear when I hope I'm not going to meet anyone I know, and we drove down to the beach. Actually, once we were out of the car and into the open air it was quite invigorating and I walked slowly along behind Tris as he scratched away looking for tiny crabs, sending up showers of sand with his busy paws. The wind had whipped up the waves into white horses and the rainy weather hid the far coast of Wales. We seemed to have the beach to ourselves apart from a pair of oyster-catchers whose distinctive plumage and bright orange beaks were a welcome, indeed a rare, sight on our bit of the coast. It was pleasant to be enclosed in a little world of our own and I felt mildly resentful when I saw another figure approaching us along the shoreline. However, as we drew nearer I saw that it was Kathy.

"Hello," I said. "I didn't think anyone else would be mad enough to be out on a day like this!"

She laughed and said, "I rather like it when it's like this and I have the beach to myself. I've always loved the sea in winter."

"Me too, though I think I prefer it when the wind's a bit less strong! So, how's everything at the surgery?"

"Oh much better now – well, you know what I mean."

"I can imagine. It must be much pleasanter to work there now you can all work together like you used to."

"It is! And even Julie – I think I told you – she seems very keen to fit in now."

"That's good. Though I did hear that she and Malcolm Hardy weren't getting on too well when he died."

"No, they had several dreadful rows. And I'm not surprised now that we know –" She stopped suddenly.

"Now that you know about the baby."

Kathy looked at me in surprise.

"You know about that?"

"Well yes, I did hear about it in a roundabout sort of way. Poor girl, it's a bad situation for her and, from what I can gather, her parents aren't being very kind."

"I know, she poured it all out to me – I can't think why."

"She needed someone to talk to and you'd be the obvious person."

"Me?"

"Yes, kind, sympathetic, not judging or blaming her. Yes, the ideal person!"

"I'm glad she did. I really felt sorry for her. All that bad behaviour when she first came – it was really Malcolm Hardy's fault, telling her how he wanted her to 'keep an eye on things' was how he put it. And she was so besotted with him. I don't think she'd had a real boyfriend before and I think, because he was much older, and what she thought of as sophisticated, she fell for him really heavily. She'd have done anything for him."

"Oh dear!"

"That's why she took it so badly, I suppose – about the baby, I mean. I don't think it occurred to her that he wouldn't be delighted, so she was absolutely shattered when he wanted her to have an abortion."

"How dreadful for her."

"Well, apparently when she told him she wouldn't he broke with her completely. You can imagine how hard it must have been for her to go on working at the surgery, but of course she had to because she needed the job."

"Surely he would have provided for the child?"

"He said how could he be sure it was his, which was completely ridiculous because she never *looked* at anyone else! Like I said, she adored him."

"So how were they, at work, I mean?"

"She wouldn't take no for an answer, so there were rows all the time, and she was often late in because she felt so rotten – but of course we none of us knew anything about this. To be honest we just thought she was being unpleasant, while all the time she was going through all that. It makes me feel really mean!"

"Well, how were you to guess? Anyway, from the way she's confided in you it looks like you've been a good friend to her now."

"I just feel sorry for her. And on top of everything else she didn't want her parents to find out – as you said, I gather they're a bit difficult, so she had to keep it all a secret and I know how hard that is."

I decided to take a chance. "Because of you and Ben?"

She gave me a startled look.

"What do you mean?"

"You and Ben," I repeated. "Having to keep that a secret."

She stood for a moment silently watching two gulls screaming overhead in a dispute over some piece of seashore detritus.

"How did you find out?"

I told her about seeing Ben at *Iolanthe*. "The expression on his face was unmistakeable," I said.

Her lips curved in a smile. "He was so sweet about that," she said. "Listen, we can't talk out here, it's too cold. Come over to the flat."

"Right. I'll just put Tris in the car, he's covered with sand."

Sitting at Kathy's kitchen table waiting for the kettle to boil I said, "Look, perhaps I shouldn't have spoken to you about Ben."

"You haven't told Mother?"

"No, of course not. Kathy, I really wasn't being interfering, it's just that I'm fond of you and I wanted, well, to sympathise I suppose. I do like Ben and I do understand how dreadfully difficult it must be for you both."

"No, I'm glad you did. It's a relief, really, to have someone I can talk to about it."

"Any time, you know that."

"The worst thing was when Malcolm Hardy found out about it."

"How awful! How did that happen?"

"I was feeling a bit low because things seemed so hopeless, you know, and Ben had his arm around me. It was out at the back in the surgery and Malcolm Hardy came in and saw us."

"So what happened?"

"Oh, he was very casual about it then, but later he used what he'd seen to blackmail Ben."

"What!"

"When he sacked him. Ben could have made things awkward – well, he'd been there a long time, there are tribunals and things – but Malcolm Hardy said that unless he went quietly he'd tell everyone about us."

"That man was even more vile than I thought!"

"Obviously I didn't want Ben's daughter to know, though he says that she'd understand, but I couldn't take the risk. And, to be honest, I didn't want Mother to hear about it. Dad would be fine I know, but..."

"Yes, I know. She won't hear about it from me. Actually, though, I think she *would* accept it, it's just that it might take a little time."

Kathy laughed. "You may be right, but I don't want to risk it – not yet at any rate. And I didn't want people to gossip about us and that sort of thing. So you do see how miserable it was for us both. When that wretched man died we both felt so relieved. Isn't that awful?"

"No," I said, "it isn't, it's quite natural – I'd certainly have felt the same. Anyway, you weren't the only ones to feel like that. He'd been making quite a few people's lives a misery."

"It's just..." She hestitated. "Just that if anyone knew about Ben and me they might think we had a motive for killing him."

"What rubbish!" I said roundly. "Anyone who knows either of you would never believe you could do anything like that, you're simply not capable of it!"

"You're my friend," Kathy said, "so you naturally think the best of us. But it *was* a motive and we were both there when it happened."

"So was Julie," I said, "and Diana, and Keith – they all had motives. Think about it."

Kathy poured the tea and handed me a cup. "I suppose so. It's just that we've both been brooding about it so much."

"You mustn't get things out of proportion," I said.

"It's hard not to. We both feel so guilty all the time."

"That's nonsense," I said firmly. "You're not hurting anyone. Ben isn't betraying his wife – the sad fact is that she doesn't exist any more as a person. And you're a free agent. All right, I know people might make snide remarks, but anyone who did wouldn't be worth bothering about. Actually, I think you *should* tell Ben's daughter. I know she loves him very much and I'm sure she'd want him to be happy. She's a sensible girl and she knows that her mother wouldn't be hurt now. It would be different if you and Ben had got together before she deteriorated, but I'm sure you

162

didn't and I think she'd understand the way things are now."

"Oh, I don't know. I couldn't bear it if she turned against her father because of me."

"I don't think she would. But perhaps if Ben sounded her out – you know, asked how she would feel if – that sort of thing, just testing the waters."

She looked doubtful. "Perhaps. I'll see what Ben thinks about it."

"I know you'd both feel better if she accepted the situation. Meanwhile," I said, "just enjoy being together!"

Kathy smiled. "It's so good – even as things are. I'm so lucky to have found him, and it's wonderful that he won't have to go away to find another job. That's why it would be so awful if anything went wrong now."

"I'm sure everything will turn out right," I said.

"Well, as I said we're lucky to have what we've got. Not like poor Julie."

"She'll have her baby."

"But no father, and how will she be able to tell the child when it's old enough to understand that its father never wanted it?"

"I know, it's a dreadful situation. But perhaps now her parents know they'll be supportive."

"Her mother's not sympathetic at all, she called her a little fool – can you imagine! And her father just wants to get any money he can out of Malcolm Hardy's estate. Poor girl, she really doesn't know which way to turn. I think she actually wants to come into work just to get away from them."

"I thought she looked quite ill the last time I saw her

at the surgery, though, of course, I didn't know then that she was pregnant."

"I don't think she's having an easy time," Kathy said. "She's been sick an awful lot and she hadn't been going for her check-ups until I made her."

"Good for you."

"I feel really sorry for her. She's made a mess of her life so young. At least I waited until I was nearly middle-aged!"

"Oh, come on. You haven't made a mess of your life and you're still young and attractive – you ask Ben!"

She laughed. "Thank you, Sheila. You really cheer me up."

"Well," I said, getting to my feet and gathering up my bag and hat, "just you remember what I said. Enjoy your life together."

When I got home, after I'd brushed the sand out of Tris's coat and off his paws, I started to make supper. Foss, who was punishing me for having been out with Tris and leaving him alone, weaved back and forth on the worktop getting in my way and dabbing his paw under the tap while I was trying to wash the potatoes. Eventually I had to shut him in the sitting-room with a handful of cat treats (and some biscuits for Tris so that *he* didn't sulk) so that I was able to get on in peace. Not just to prepare the food, but also to consider my conversation with Kathy.

It was obvious that she and Ben were very much in love and she was right, it did (given that Malcolm Hardy had tried to blackmail Ben) mean that they had a motive for murdering him. I had seen for myself the intensity of Ben's feelings for her and today I'd realised just how deeply she cared for him. Still, I knew – I really *knew* – that Kathy wasn't capable of such a thing. But, given all the circumstances, could I be equally sure about Ben?

Chapter Fourteen

For some maddening reason I couldn't find my Christmas card list. I usually take down the cards, list their senders and put the list and cards away in an old shoe box until I need them next year. It is one of my few bits of proper organisation and I've always been rather proud of it. But although the cards were there in the shoe box (on the top of the wardrobe in the spare room along with the box containing practically every Christmas decorations we've ever had since Michael was a child) there was no sign of the list. If I was going to know how many cards to buy – time was getting on and the best charity cards always seem to get snapped up by the middle of November nowadays – it looked as though I was going to have to go through the cards again and make a new list. With a sigh I began looking through them. It is always interesting to match the card to the sender. Usually one can guess the sort of card each person will send; Old Master reproductions of the Nativity from some, designer angels in mauve and silver from others, quite a few snow scenes (though I can't remember when we last had a white Christmas in Taviscombe), many "jolly" cards, with anthropomorphic penguins, polar bears and geese, and, of course, the occasional Santa Claus, divorced from his St Nicholas persona and usually in the company of cartoon-type reindeer. Occasionally though, there is a surprise. My usually austere cousin Hilda, for example, abandoning the habits of a lifetime (a tasteful Raphael or Rubens), had, under the profound influence of the new love of her life (a cat called Tolly), sent me a card featuring a Siamese wearing a Santa Claus hat and carrying a sack full of toys appearing round the side of a chimney. The message (in silver glitter lettering) read "Have a miaouwvellous Christmas". I put it aside with a smile and continued my task.

Foss, who had somehow insinuated himself into the room, came to assist me by sitting on the table and hooking out cards from the pile and sweeping them onto the floor.

"Oh Foss," I exclaimed, "don't *do* that! You're as bad as Toby!"

I got up and put him outside again, but after I'd done so a thought struck me so that I sat motionless, Rosemary's card (a view of the Taviscombe lifeboat at sea) still held in my hand.

Was it possible, I thought, that for an as yet undiscovered reason, Malcolm Hardy had in some form or other administered the insulin to *himself*? No phial or syringe had been found, of course, but what if Toby, in his usual way, had leapt up on the desk and knocked it onto the floor? It might easily have rolled underneath something where it could have lain undiscovered, and, indeed, might be there still. I racked my brains to think of some reason for Malcolm Hardy to have done such a thing but my medical knowledge wasn't great enough for me to hazard even a guess. I put the thought away from me and went on with my list but the idea kept nagging away so that eventually I picked up the phone and spoke to Roger. I told him my theory very tentatively expecting a polite but sceptical reply but to my surprise he seemed to think it worth consideration.

"The fact is," he said ruefully, "we've been getting nowhere. All our lines of enquiry seem to come to nothing. To be honest I'm really clutching at straws."

"You know about Julie and the baby, I suppose?"

"Yes, but that doesn't seem to lead anywhere. I suppose she might have killed him for revenge or something melodramatic like that, but, from what I can gather, she wasn't the sort of girl who'd have the *initiative* to do anything about it!"

I smiled at his choice of words and said, "So you think that it might be possible that for some reason, he took it himself?"

"It's worth considering. I'll have to get a medical opinion, of course. But one thing I can do," he added with sudden resolution, "is to go and have another look at that surgery."

Roger came round to see me late the following afternoon.

"You were right," he said.

"Really?"

"Well, insofar as there *was* something there. It wasn't a phial or a syringe, but something almost as good."

"Come on tell me!" I exclaimed.

"There wasn't anything in any of the examination rooms or whatever they're called," Roger said, "but we did have more luck in Malcolm Hardy's office. Fortunately one of the people who do the general cleaning has been off sick for a while so this particular office has been left pretty well untouched."

"Yes?"

"There's a large rather heavy desk in there and when we moved it we found a hip flask. Presumably," he added giving me a quizzical look, "put there by that cat."

"I expect," I said, "Toby jumped onto the desk and batted it onto the floor and then pushed it underneath."

"It would seem likely. Anyway, the flask is silver with his initials on so it is definitely his – quite light-weight when empty, which it was when we found it."

"So?"

"So I don't think we have to look any further for the source of the alcohol that was found in his body."

"What did it have in it?"

"Just a few drains of liquid, probably whisky – at least that's what it smelled like. I've sent it off to be analysed."

"Does it help?" I asked.

Roger smiled. "It means that we don't have to go round any more pubs looking for where he had his last drink, and it clears up a loose end, but no, I suppose it doesn't get the actual investigation any further forward."

"I'm sorry."

"No, it was a good thought on your part and if by any chance there's anything other than whisky found in the flask that may help, though it's not likely that they'll find traces of insulin in there now after all this time."

"Oh dear, what a pity. Maddening to have *found* something and then it's no use! Oh well, have you got time for a cup of tea?"

"No, I'd better be getting back, I only called in because I was passing the end of your lane."

"You'll let me know if the forensic people find any-thing in the flask?"

"Of course."

"Give my love to Delia and the children."

As I stood on the step waving goodbye I had mixed feelings. A sort of triumph that I had been right about Toby and a distinct feeling of let-down over what had actually been found. A muffled miaow made me look down and I saw Foss, who had been off hunting, coming across the front lawn with a mouse in his mouth. Since, like all Siamese, he feels that he has the inalienable right to eat anything he catches on his own dish in the kitchen, I shut the door hurriedly on him before he could bring his trophy indoors. I knew that when I opened the door again I would find nothing left of the mouse but a pathetic little gall bladder (presumably inedible) laid out on the door mat. Wishing, once more, that cats were herbivores, I went into the kitchen to make myself the cup of tea I now felt I needed.

Michael phoned a little later on.

"I've picked up your computer from Dave so, if you like, I'll come round after work and set it up for you."

"That would be marvellous," I said thankfully.

When Michael arrived with the computer I left him to it. I find that anyone with more knowledge of computers than I have (which is more or less everybody) has this irresistible urge to *explain* things to me. The fact is, I just want the thing to work – I really don't care *how* it does it. Also Michael is always wanting to put refinements on mine ("I've given you this new screen saver, I thought you'd like it better than the other one, and I've put some new icons for you so that you've got short cuts...") and if I'm there in the room I have to stand patiently beside him while he fiddles with lists of things that flash up and down the screen, inducing dizziness and, finally, a splitting headache. It isn't that I'm not grateful. I am. But I just want the end result not the detail.

"There now," Michael said, coming back into the kitchen. "I've set it up for you and everything seems to be fine. Dave's given you a lot more memory and a new modem and tidied things up a bit, so you should be all right now."

"Did you manage to get an invoice out of him?" I asked. Dave is always reluctant to accept payment because he is so passionate about what he does he obviously he feels that *he* should pay his customers for providing him with lovely problems to work on.

"Yes – far too little of course. I've left it by the computer."

"Oh good, I'll send him a cheque. Would you like a cup of tea or a drink or anything?"

"No, I'd better be getting back – Alice's bedtime and all that."

I smiled fondly. "She's a lucky child to have such doting parents. Not like Julie's baby, poor little thing. Is there any more news on that front?"

"Not really. One thing, though. We felt we had to tell June Hardy about the baby."

"Really?"

"It only seemed fair."

"So how did she take it?"

"She seemed more stunned than anything. We explained that nothing would be done until the baby had actually been born – so of course probate will be delayed – and she understood that."

"Poor June, it seems so wretched that she should get

nothing yet again. It must have been a blow when her father died, but this time it seems doubly unfair. I mean, that someone like Julie, not even connected to the family, someone who was with Malcolm Hardy for such a short time, should get the lot. Isn't there any way she could get *something*?"

"Well, she could contest the will of course, but it's a long and unsatisfactory business and we wouldn't advise her (as friends as well as solicitors) to go along that course."

"Oh well, she's got a job that she loves and no one to leave the money to when she goes, so I suppose it's all right."

"June's a sensible person, I'm sure she'll settle for the life she's got."

"At least," I said, "she won't have to decide what stuff to keep and what to get rid of in that ghastly house. I told you, didn't I, what a mammoth task *that* will be. I suppose Julie will have to do all that now. Do you think *she'll* want to live there?"

"Surely not. It'll fetch a good round sum – there's all that ground as well."

"I expect her horrible father will expect to live off the proceeds for the rest of his life. She doesn't sound like the sort of girl who'll stand up to him."

"Probably not. Well, that's all in the future. Oh, by the way, Thea said would you mind coming to us for Christmas? I know we usually come here, but with Alice and all her stuff it would be easier with us. She said it was time you had a rest from cooking Christmas lunch after all these years!"

"Yes, of course, it'll be lovely. I'll give her a ring tomorrow."

When Michael had gone I poured myself a glass of sherry although it was earlier than my usual time. Of course it made sense for me to go to the children for Christmas and it was silly to feel just a little bit sad that I wouldn't be making the puddings (it was nearly Stir-up Sunday), stuffing the turkey while I listened to Carols from Kings' or decorating the big Christmas tree. On an impulse I got up and went to fetch the box of decorations from on top of the wardrobe and lifted out, one by one, the ornaments we have always had on the tree. I lingered especially over a pair of glass reindeer. I remembered Michael, aged two, exclaiming with delight as he saw them glittering as the fairy lights went on and off, and stretching out his tiny hands as if he could catch the reflections from them. I sat there for quite a while remembering. Then I pulled myself together, put the ornaments away and finished my glass of sherry.

"Oh dear," I said to Tris who had come to sit by my feet in front of the fire. "It's silly to keep thinking about the past. Perhaps Dave could take *away* some of my memory!"

Tris raised his head and looked at me, but deciding that no reply was called for, rested it again on my foot and went back to sleep.

I saw June Hardy a few days later and we stopped for a little chat. I wasn't going to say anything about Julie and the will but she mentioned it. She told me briefly what had happened and went on, "So I'm afraid all the splendid work you and Anthea did, sorting things out and putting labels on them, was all wasted."

"Perhaps not," I said tentatively. "Perhaps this girl will want to get rid of some of them."

She gave a short laugh. "Oh, I'm sure she will, but I don't imagine she'll give them to the Red Cross auction, do you?"

"Probably not. Actually, I don't know the girl – at least I've seen her briefly at the surgery, but that's about all. What's she like?"

"I don't really know. I've never met her, but from what I've gathered she was completely under Malcolm's thumb. You probably know that his mother was very possessive and he didn't have any serious girlfriends whilst she was alive. I suppose he felt obliged to make up for it after she was dead. He certainly went off the rails then, anyway!"

"Really?"

"Oh yes, this Julie was the last of a long line of girls. I imagine he would have got rid of her just as he got rid of all the others if he'd lived long enough"

"Well, from what I heard he did. He didn't want her to keep the baby because he'd already started a relationship with someone else. Claudia Drummond – do you know her?"

June gave an exclamation of disgust. "But she's a married woman! Her husband's Sir Robert Drummond, he's very distinguished. I worked with him at Bristol when I was a theatre sister there."

"Did you?"

"Oh yes." Her face softened. "Such a nice man, always so courteous – not all consultants are you know – and so considerate. I remember we were all very upset when we heard about his marriage. It was obviously never going to work, she was so much younger

175

than he was. They met in South Africa. I suppose things seem different when you're abroad."

"Actually it seems that she had also finished with Malcolm, on the day that he died."

She seemed not to have heard me and said, "Poor Sir Robert, he deserved better than that."

Since it appeared that in her eyes Sir Robert could do no wrong I didn't mention his apparent complaisance about his wife's affairs but returned to the subject I found more interesting.

"When's Julie's baby due, do you know?" I asked.

"Sometime in the spring, I believe. I don't know exactly."

"I'm so sorry. It must be awful for you."

She gave me a brief smile. "I would have liked to think that justice had been done after the iniquity of my father's will, but, obviously that was not to be."

"Still..."

"It's very kind of you to be concerned, Sheila, but it is not a subject I wish to dwell on."

"No, of course not."

"I must be getting on. I have to take Mr Lindsay to see about his hearing aid and I've got a mass of paperwork waiting for me at the Larches. We're having a few problems at the moment and it all needs sorting out."

"Yes of course. Oh, by the way, I've been meaning to ask you, how is Ben Turner's wife?"

"Elizabeth Turner? Well, actually, I'm a little worried about her. It's her heart, you know? Basically angina but she did have a nasty attack last week. Dr Macdonald says she should be all right but we have to monitor her very carefully – check her medication and so forth. With Alzheimers, as you can imagine, you have to keep a very sharp eye on things, make sure that she actually takes everything when she should."

"Goodness," I said. "I do think you're wonderful!"

June smiled. "It's a job," she said, "and it's one that I enjoy. Now I must be getting on."

I crossed the road and went into the library because I'd got quite cold standing talking to June. As I stood in the biography section staring mindlessly at the shelves I thought of Elizabeth Turner, locked into her solitary world of Alzheimers, and wondered if perhaps it would be the kindest thing for a heart attack to carry her off. And I wondered how many times Ben and Kathy might have had the same thought, and, good souls that they were, how many times they must have felt guilty about having felt just a glimmer of hope.

When I got back the phone was ringing. It was Thea.

"Sheila," she said, "could I ask you a great favour? Could you *very* kindly make one of your Christmas puddings for us all – and the Christmas cake too? I'm sorry to bother you – I did want you to have a good rest this year, but what with Alice..."

"Of course," I said. "I'd love to!"

"Oh thank you, that's marvellous. There is something else. Michael said would you mind bringing over the Christmas tree ornaments? It seems that he won't feel it's a proper Christmas without them! He said something about two glass reindeer..."

Chapter Fifteen

In a way I quite like Christmas shopping; that is in the early stages while I'm still relatively fresh and not in a last minute panic. I'd made a sort of tentative list (nothing set in stone, I could change my mind if I saw something nicer) for Michael, Thea and Alice. This year everyone else, I had decided, would be having flowers or something to eat sent by post.

We're not really very well off for shops in Taviscombe. Of course we're lucky to have two supermarkets for food and so on and we've got a couple of marvellous butchers and a farm shop, but an awful lot of the shops, as in most seaside towns, just have stuff for holiday makers, either 'fancy' gift shops or basic stores full of tat that are, in any case, boarded up for the winter.

I rang up Rosemary.

"How do you feel about a day's shopping in Taunton?" I asked.

"Won't it be a bit crowded with Christmas shoppers?"

"Probably, but the longer we leave it the worse it'll be. And there are some things I want that I simply can't get here."

"All right. Will tomorrow be all right? It's a Tuesday – surely not many people shop on a Tuesday."

Unfortunately everyone else seemed to have the same view of that particular day of the week and I had a dreadful time trying to find somewhere to park, but we both managed to find things we wanted so the expedition and the hassle was worthwhile.

"Let's not have lunch in the town," Rosemary said after we had looked for ages in the usual cafes and found them uncomfortably full of weary shoppers, the floor space around each table cluttered with large carrier bags. "Let's try a pub on the way home."

When we got to The Farmers Arms that was quite crowded too, but we found a table at the back and ordered some food. I had just embarked on my paté when Rosemary nudged me.

"That alcove at the back," she whispered. "Look who's there!"

I tried to turn unobtrusively and saw Keith and Julie Barnes. Actually I could have had a good stare and they wouldn't have noticed since they were very much occupied with each other.

"Goodness," I said. "Who'd have thought it!"

"It must be serious," Rosemary said. "After all she's quite noticeably pregnant."

"Keith always struck me as a nice boy," I said. "Perhaps he's just sorry for her."

"It looks like a bit more than sorry. Anyway, I thought no one at the surgery liked her."

"Apparently she's been quite different since she split up with Malcolm Hardy – even before he died, I think. Kathy says she was really a nice girl but entirely under his influence and sort of dazzled by what she took to be his sophisticated lifestyle."

"Good heavens. I didn't think there were any girls like that around anymore."

"And from what I can gather Keith's always been a bit shy and hasn't had a serious girlfriend. I think it's rather sweet."

"Perhaps they don't want people to know," Rosemary

said thoughtfully. "I mean, they're pretty well tucked away out of sight back there, aren't they?"

But while we were having our coffee they passed our table on the way out and Keith stopped and spoke to me.

"Hello, Mrs Malory, fancy seeing you here!"

"We've been shopping," I said, "and Taunton was too crowded to eat in. It's nice here, do you come often?"

"Actually, someone I know has just taken the place over so I thought we'd come and see how he was getting on."

"It seems to be doing well," I said. "I can't remember when I've seen it so full at lunchtime."

"Well," Rosemary said when they'd gone. "Fancy that."

"It never pays," I said, "to jump to conclusions."

"They certainly seem to be an item, though. Do you want another cup of coffee or shall we go?"

I was curious to know what Kathy made of this new development but I didn't see her by chance in the town and, after our talk about Ben, I felt reluctant to ring her up in case she thought I was trying to force confidences out of her. I did, however, find myself next to Anthea in the queue at the supermarket checkout. It was a long queue and Anthea was very cross about it.

"Just look," she said scornfully, "at people doing their Christmas food shopping *now*! No wonder the place is so crowded."

The woman in front, whose trolley contained dates, satsumas, boxes of crackers and a large Christmas pudding, stiffened but pretended she hadn't heard the comment.

"When we were young," Anthea continued, "it was all done in the last week – I remember always going out with my father and sister on Christmas Eve to buy my mother's present. That was the *real* Christmas spirit! Now it all starts in October and children have Advent calendars with *chocolates* when they open each door. I can't believe it sometimes."

"Are you all going to Jean's for Christmas?" I asked, anxious to introduce a topic of conversation less offensive to the woman in front of us.

"Oh no," Anthea said. "Jean wanted us to, she said the boys liked to have their presents at home, but I told her that I've always done Christmas for us all and I have no intention of giving up now! Besides, when would she have time to do everything – do it properly I mean – when she's got her job and everything?"

"It will be a lot of work for you," I said.

"Oh, Kathy will help me. She always does the vegetables and the bread sauce, and sees to the table."

"That's nice."

"I think I told you how much better she's been since that dreadful man died."

"Yes, when I saw her last she looked very well."

"The whole set-up at the surgery is fine now the police have stopped harassing them. They seem to have dropped the whole thing, at least I haven't heard anything, and a good thing too. The world's a much better place without him!"

The woman in front was agog now and visibly straining to hear our conversation.

"Yes, well, it's nice to see the girls there so relaxed again."

"And have you heard the latest? That girl Julie, you

know the one who's supposed to be having *his* baby, she's only gone and got herself engaged!"

"Really?"

"Yes, to young Keith. I couldn't believe it when Kathy told me. Why he wants to go and saddle himself with another man's child I can't imagine. He seemed such a nice young man."

The queue had now moved forward and the woman in front was obliged (reluctantly I thought) to get the things out of her trolley and go to the far end of the checkout, obviously deeply frustrated at not hearing the end of the story.

"It will be good for the baby to have a father, poor little thing," I said.

"I suppose so," Anthea said grudgingly. "Still it does seem a waste somehow."

I wondered if, in spite of the age difference between them, she had earmarked Keith for Kathy.

"She sounds a rather silly girl," Anthea went on, shovelling her purchases onto the moving belt. "There's no excuse for a girl to get herself into trouble in this day and age. It was different years ago – in fact they do say Cynthia Burton *had* to marry that man Barnes because this girl was on the way."

"Nobody *has* to marry anyone nowadays," I said.

"More's the pity!" Anthea said, signing her credit card slip with a flourish. "All these single parents – no wonder the crime rate's what it is."

"Well there's one baby that won't be having a single parent now," I said.

"True, and I suppose it's better that it should be brought up by someone as steady as Keith rather than by that dreadful Malcolm Hardy."

183

She stood and waited impatiently while I piled the bags of groceries into my trolley.

"Oh, I don't think Malcolm Hardy would have had anything to do with bringing it up," I said as we emerged from the store. "I believe he wanted Julie to get rid of it. They split up because she wouldn't – at least, he wouldn't have anything else to do with her."

"Have an abortion!" Anthea stood stock still in the middle of the car park so that an elderly man driving an old Fiesta had to swerve to avoid her. "But that's dreadful! That poor girl! I wouldn't be surprised if *she* killed him. I know I would have!"

"There's no reason to suppose she did," I said. "Anyway, she doesn't sound like the sort of girl who'd do a thing like that."

"Who knows what *anyone* is capable of," Anthea said darkly, "if the circumstances are powerful enough, and goodness knows they were in this case."

"Well, I don't think..."

"Anyway," Anthea said firmly, tying the plastic bags securely before putting them away in the boot of her car. "If she *did* kill him, I for one wouldn't blame her."

As I drove away I turned Anthea's theory (if such it could be called) over in my mind. Certainly, what I had heard about Julie didn't lead me to believe that she would be capable of actually killing someone, especially in such a calculated way. On the other hand, she must have been in a highly emotional state and full of resentment and, perhaps, revenge. On my way home I went down to the sea wall, a place I often go when I want to think about something. I parked the car and walked a little way, disturbing the flock of seagulls roosting on the rails, who rose in a cloud and hovered hopefully in case I might be going to throw food for them, then settled back again on their perches or down on the shingle below. It was quite a mild day with no wind and everything was quiet so that I could hear the swish of waves on the pebbles as they end-lessly advanced and retreated.

I wished I actually knew Julie, or at least that I'd had more than a brief exchange with her at the surgery, so that I could form my own opinion of what she might or might not be capable of. A simple girl, Kathy had said, easily influenced, easily impressed, but a girl, nevertheless, who had been unpleasant to her work-mates and had spied on them for her lover. She had also lied to her parents, though that was perhaps not surprising given the circumstances and their lack of sympathy.

It suddenly occurred to me that she might have known about old Mr Hardy's will. It was just possible that Malcolm might have mentioned it in some con-text or other. If she *had* known about it, then she would have had a very good motive for killing him. Malcolm would be dead and his child (and the child's mother at least for the early years) would inherit a great deal of money. It certainly was a motive; I wondered if Roger had considered it. It also occurred to me that if Julie could establish the child's paternity (and there seemed to be very little doubt that it was Malcolm Hardy's) then not only would she be very well off, but that Keith, when they were married, would also share in the good fortune.

I wondered when Keith and Julie had first got together. Was it, in fact before Malcolm Hardy's death?

Had Julie confided in him and how had he reacted? Could he...? My mind shied away from the thought but I resolutely brought it back. Could he have *helped* Julie to kill her former lover? I immediately rejected the idea, but somehow I kept coming back to it. After all – Keith and Julie, it was an unexpected combination. Was there a more sinister reason for it than simple need on one side and sympathy on the other?

I saw a small figure approaching. It was an old friend of my mother, Mrs Patterson, walking her dog, as she always did at this time of the afternoon. As she drew near I saw that the King Charles spaniel was limping and had a bandage on one of his front legs.

"Oh dear," I said, when we had exchanged greetings and commented on the unseasonable mildness of the weather, "is Benjy all right?"

"He's better now," she replied, bending down to pat him, "aren't you, poor boy? But he had a nasty cut on his leg. Some dreadful boys riding their bicycles on the pavement! They came up behind us – I didn't hear a thing – and gave poor Benjy a terrible knock."

"That's really disgraceful!"

"What can you do? They're out of control. I called after them but they took absolutely no notice and I was too worried about Benjy to do anything else."

"You managed to get him to the vet all right?"

"Oh yes. By a merciful coincidence, Mr Sully, you know, he lives two doors down from me, was passing so he took us there in his car – so good, he waited and took us home as well."

"So what did the vet say?"

"It was that nice young man Keith. He was *so* kind. When I told him what had happened he said that *I'd* had a shock as well as my poor boy here, so he got one of the girls to make me a cup of tea."

"That was very thoughtful."

"Oh he is! When my poor Barny had to be put down – he was the one I had before Benjy – he came to the house to do it and was *so* kind and understanding. Well, he checked that there was nothing broken and bound the paw up and now Benjy is *much* better. Well, you see he wants to go for his usual walk so he must be feeling well!"

I smiled. "That must be such a relief for you."

"Oh it was. You see Benjy is all I've got since Arthur died and now that Tony's gone to live in Dundee."

Tony is her son and, to my mind, doesn't give his mother the attention she deserves.

"Will you see him at Christmas?" I asked.

"Well, they did invite me, Tony and Fiona, and I would like to see the children, but I really don't think I can manage the journey and, in any case, I couldn't take Benjy – Fiona doesn't care for animals. No, I shall be having Christmas lunch with my friend Doreen – you remember Doreen Vasey, I'm sure – we'll go to a hotel so that neither of us will have to cook. And what about you, my dear? That precious little girl's first Christmas – I was so pleased they gave her your dear mother's name."

"Yes, I'll be going to them for Christmas. It should be great fun."

Benjy gave a little whine and held up his injured paw, reminding his mistress that no one was paying attention to him.

"Oh look at him, the little love," Mrs Patterson exclaimed. "Telling me to stop chattering on!"

I watched them out of sight and then walked slowly back to my car.

I was having supper with Michael and Thea that evening and I tentatively told them my theory about Julie.

"Well, I suppose she *might* have done it," Thea said. "After all, she must have been feeling dreadful, especially if, as you say, she was completely besotted with the ghastly man and then he let her down so badly just when she needed support over the baby."

"And, of course," I said, "she probably knew by then about his carrying on with Claudia Drummond."

"Exactly."

"Mind you," I continued, "from what I've seen of her she doesn't look capable of doing anything as positive as killing someone."

"What was it old Mrs Mac used to say?" Michael said. "'Even a worm will turn if it's trod on'? Possibly the worm turned."

"Or," I added, "she may have had help."

I told them about the engagement and the possibility that she and Keith might have managed it between them.

"Mmm, I don't know," Michael said. "Surely the timing's a bit tricky. Would there have been time for that relationship to have developed before Malcolm Hardy died?"

"It's just possible," I said, "that Keith was in love with her *before* Malcolm Hardy behaved in such a caddish way and he leapt at the chance of being her knight in shining armour."

"Possible, I suppose. Does that sound like him?" Thea asked. "I've only seen him a couple of times when I took Smoke for injections, so I don't know what he's really like."

"That's just it," I admitted. "It's not like him at all. Well, the knight-in-shining-armour bit is, but he's such a kindly soul and he's so marvellous with animals, so gentle – he really loves them."

"Oh come on, Ma," Michael said. "A love of animals doesn't necessarily mean anyone's whiter than white. After all Hitler liked dogs!"

"I know that, of course, but no, I can't believe Keith had anything to do with the murder."

"But you think Julie might have?" Thea asked.

"I really don't know. Like everyone else at the surgery, she had the means, she *could* have done it."

"Oh well, I'll just go and see how the food is doing. Do you feel like giving Alice her bath?"

As I gently rubbed shampoo into my granddaughter's hair while she tried to catch the bubbles in the water, and laughed as they slipped through her fingers, I decided that this was more important than theories about a murder that didn't really concern me and gave all my mind to the intricacies of a game that Alice liked to play with her plastic ducks and the loofah.

Chapter Sixteen

When I heard the clicking noise Tris's claws made on the tiled floor of the kitchen I realised that it was time to take him to have his nails cut. I was able to get an appointment with Diana, though when I got there I had to wait quite a while until she was free and when I finally saw her I thought she looked decidedly flustered.

"Sorry to keep you waiting," she said, "but it's a bit hectic this afternoon. I mean, it's lovely that we're so busy but we are one person short these days."

"Yes, it must be difficult for you."

"And to make things worse," Diana went on picking up the clippers, "Julie is off at the moment."

"Oh dear, what's the matter?"

"She had a bad fall."

"How dreadful. Is she all right? What about the baby?"

"They're both OK, but they're keeping her in hospital for a bit to be on the safe side."

She picked up another of Tris's paws and began to clip the nails.

"She must have been lucky," I said.

"Keith was with her and he called an ambulance straight away."

"Oh yes, Keith – I was quite surprised to hear about the engagement."

Diana looked at me quizzically. "You're not the only one," she said. "We were all amazed."

"They never seemed to be particularly close?" I enquired tentatively.

"Not that I was aware, but then there was that business with Malcolm..." She broke off, presumably aware of the impropriety of discussing the affairs of one of her employees.

"Right then, there's the nails done." She ruffled Tris's ears affectionately. "Is there anything else?"

"Oh yes please, if you wouldn't mind giving him a general look-over – ears, teeth, heart and so on. It's always such a business getting him here that we might as well do the job properly now he is!"

While she was examining him I asked, "Have you been able to find someone to replace Malcolm Hardy?"

"We've got a locum coming in next week but nothing definite's been decided."

"It must have been awkward for you, having the police around and so forth."

"Yes, it's been awful. And they still don't seem to have got much further with the affair. They keep coming back to look at this and that and ask more questions. It's very unsettling for everybody."

"I can imagine."

"I mean, there's no way anyone here would have done a thing like that! You know us all, Mrs Malory, can you believe any of *us* could be a murderer?"

Her voice rose slightly and I realised just how much she must have been under stress.

"No, of course not!" I said warmly. "And I'm sure no one would ever think such a thing."

She smiled faintly at my vehemence. "Thank you. I'm sorry, what must you think of me? It's just that the whole thing is getting to me – the fact of it still going on and no solution yet."

"It must have been a dreadful strain," I said,

"especially for you. After all it's your practice. I can see that you really do need to have it cleared up. I'm sure everybody must feel for you."

"Thank you." She picked up her stethoscope and listened for a moment to Tris's heart and then smiled and patted his head.

"There's a good boy. No, he's in very good shape for a dog of his age. You are watching his diet, aren't you? Extra weight does put a strain on the heart and I know it's very tempting to give him tit-bits."

When I got back to the waiting room it was empty so I was able to have a little chat with Alison while I was paying my bill.

"I was sorry to hear about Julie," I said. "How did it happen?"

Alison waited until the computer had disgorged my bill and then came back and leaned on the counter.

"Well," she said, "four of us – Julie and Keith and me and my boyfriend Ian – went to the Dunster by Candlelight thing. You know, the shopping evening. It's very pretty, all the decorations and the candles, all the shops lit up."

"How lovely," I said.

"They had carols and the morris dancers too," Alison went on, "it was really nice and of course it's very popular. The trouble was it did get very crowded and after a bit Ian and I got separated from the other two so we didn't actually see what happened."

"Perhaps," I suggested, "it wasn't a very suitable place for Julie to go. In her condition, I mean."

"That's what I thought, but she was so keen. Anyway, apparently they were going down that hilly bit, you know where the pavement is cobbled – quite dangerous at the best of times – and it had been raining so the cobbles were slippery, and what with so many people! Keith said someone in the crowd must have jostled her and she fell down. They thought at first she was all right, but then she started to get pains so Keith called an ambulance on his mobile."

"How dreadful!"

"We'd caught up with them by then and when the ambulance arrived Keith went with her to hospital. They took her to Taunton so we went on after to bring Keith back because he'd left his car in Dunster car park."

"Goodness, what a night you must have had."

"Well, we waited with him at the hospital because of course he wanted to see how she was."

"She was very lucky not to lose the baby," I said.

"I know." She paused for a moment and then she said, "It's funny really, Keith seemed even more relieved about that than Julie. I mean she was pleased, but he seemed, well I don't know, he seemed *really* thankful."

"I expect he was just pleased for her," I suggested.

"I suppose so, but after all, it's not even his baby. Mind you, I think he's quite happy about that for various reasons."

"Really?"

"Well, you see, he doesn't have any family himself."

"No one?"

"No. Both his parents were killed in an accident when he was a child and he was brought up by his grandmother and she's dead now, so he doesn't have a soul. So I think he'll be pleased to have a ready-made family, if you see what I mean."

"Poor Keith. Well, I do hope it works out for him."

Toby the three-legged cat suddenly materialised and leapt onto the counter between us, rubbing his head against Alison's arm and miaouing.

"Wants something to eat," Alison said, "don't you, you old fraud? Pretending to be half starved, when I know Kathy fed you before she went off only an hour ago!"

I picked up my bill and wrote the cheque.

"Right, and I must take Tris home. He's been very good but there's a limit to his patience!"

Hearing his name Tris gave a little whine. Toby leaned over the counter, gave him a scornful stare and stalked off towards the back, presumably in search of food.

I thought about what Alison had said while I was getting supper. The fact that Keith had been so relieved when Julie's baby was all right. Of course, it might have been natural concern for Julie and, indeed, it probably was, and yet... *Could* he have known about the terms of the Hardy Trust? But, even if he did, there was no evidence that he had anything to do with Malcolm Hardy's murder. It was odd though that he'd become engaged to Julie so soon after Malcolm's death – a simple girl (so Kathy said) and easily influenced, with no support at home and glad to have someone to rely on. A young, attractive man (why had he not already got a girlfriend?) with a sympathetic manner; it wasn't surprising that she had turned to him.

I whisked the butter and sugar together vigorously as if to dispel these thoughts, but they wouldn't go away. It could be that *if* Keith had known about the disposition of the Hardy fortune he was interested in the money but hadn't been connected with the death. But then *who* had killed Malcolm Hardy? It all came back to that in the end, and I was no nearer than Roger was to solving that particular mystery.

I was suddenly impatient with *all* my activities. I looked down at the small dariole mould that I'd filled with jam and the sponge mixture and I wondered why I was going to all this trouble to make a pudding just for myself. For a moment a feeling of depression and loneliness swept over me. Then I pulled myself together.

"Don't be so ridiculous!" I said out loud.

At the sound of my voice, Tris came trotting into the kitchen, closely followed by Foss, anxious not to miss anything. They sat at my feet looking up at me hopefully and I laughed and put the mould into the steamer, gave them each a handful of treats and went to pour myself a glass of sherry.

For the next few days I was too busy to concern myself with any sort of mystery; no time, indeed, to think of anything except the matter in hand. The editor of a journal to which I occasionally contributed unexpectedly sent me a book to review. Her usual reviewer had let her down and it was almost press day and, since I was an old friend, could I *possibly* help her out and she *really* needed it within the week. She knew that it was an *impossible* thing to ask anyone, but I was so good and so *quick* and it need only be quite a *short* review, just a notice really, but she did feel they had to cover it in some way and she'd be *eternally* grateful...

I approached the task with some misgivings. The

book was not only not in my field but was also long, turgid and crammed with information, some of which, unfortunately, was new and important, but which had to be sifted from the surrounding dross and evaluated conscientiously. To make life even more difficult it had all its footnotes at the back so I was continuously turning back and forth in the book until my patience was stretched almost to breaking point. In one chapter the author devoted several pages to the Temperance Movement and the evils of drink among the lower classes in Victorian society and, as I read it, a tiny thought leapt into my mind, but I pushed it resolutely to one side while I concentrated on my task.

However, when I had finished the book and (with some difficulty) written the review, I did allow myself to think about it. The hip flask that Roger had recently found, surely that might have been the source of the insulin as well as the alcohol? It would surely have been possible for someone to put it in the flask. Someone outside the surgery. It opened up a whole new range of possibilities and I wondered if Roger had considered them.

Michael came round after work – I had to send my review by e-mail and, although I could manage a short e-mail letter, I wasn't confident of my ability to send something as complicated as that.

"It's perfectly simple, Ma," Michael said. "I've told you heaps of times how to do it!"

"Well, darling, don't tell me again – just *do* it."

With a sigh and with a sort of running commentary on what he was doing he set to work.

"You see – copy and cut – perfectly easy – *then* log on to your e-mail thingy and *paste* and then send it. We could have sent it as an attachment of course..." He looked at me watching him anxiously. "No, perhaps we'll leave that for now. There now – log off, OK? Did you get that?"

"Yes," I lied, knowing perfectly well that I hadn't been concentrating. "Michael, I've had an idea about the Hardy case."

Michael switched off the computer and sighed.

"I knew you weren't paying any attention to what I was saying! Go on then, what is it?"

I told him about my idea about the hip flask. "You see, I never really thought that any of the people at the surgery could be a murderer. This means it could have been anybody!"

"Someone we've never heard of, you mean?"

"Possibly. He may have had enemies we know nothing about. Or," I hesitated, "it *could* have been Claudia Drummond. "

"Your *bête noir*?"

"Well, you must admit she's a nasty piece of work."

"But didn't Roger rule her out?"

"Only because he didn't think Malcolm Hardy would have stopped to have a drink with her after the furious row they had. But she could have put something in the flask *before* they had the quarrel."

"How exactly?"

"Well, let me see. I expect the flask was in his jacket pocket, he could have taken his jacket off and put it down somewhere."

"It's winter, for goodness sake," Michael protested. "Why would he want to take his jacket off?"

"I expect the central heating would have been turned up," I said. "After all she is from South Africa.

Anyway, if she wanted to do the deadly deed she wouldn't have told him straight away that she was breaking with him, she'd have tried to make him relax, she'd have cosied up to him."

"What a revolting phrase – you've been watching too much television!"

"So," I continued, ignoring the interruption, "he'd have taken off his jacket and then when he was out of the room for a moment –"

"Why would he go out of the room?"

"I don't know," I snapped. "Perhaps she asked him to open a bottle of wine in the kitchen or something – don't be difficult – then when he was out of the way she put the stuff in his hip flask. *Then* she started the row, to get him out of the way."

"Yes?"

"And she knew that when he was all wound up he'd need to have a drink – and *voilà!*"

"It's all very well saying *voilà* like that," Michael said, "but it's all the most extreme kind of speculation."

"But it's possible?"

"Well yes, it's *possible*, on a flying pig level."

"Even if it wasn't Claudia," I said, "there's no reason why it shouldn't be someone else – someone from outside the practice."

"It could be I suppose..."

"Anyway, I think I'll give Roger a ring and see what he thinks."

"He'll probably laugh at you," Michael said.

But when I did ring Roger he listened carefully to what I had to say.

"Perhaps my theory about Claudia is a bit far-fetched," I said tentatively.

199

"It's a possibility," Roger said, "and we must consider every possibility after all. And it *is* possible that the hip flask may have contained more than whisky."

"I suppose he filled it from one of those bottles at his home," I said. "Anthea and I were very struck by the amount and variety of alcohol there." And I told him about our morning of labelling things for June.

Roger laughed. "I can imagine Anthea's reaction."

"And to the bedroom," I said. "She was absolutely horrified at that – so much so that she refused to go right into the room, but only stood on the threshold, disapprovingly."

"It was certainly – unusual," Roger said.

"You checked the house, I suppose."

"Oh yes. Though now we'll have to go back and check the whisky bottles more thoroughly. There should be enough traces left in the flask for the forensic people to see if it came from one of his own bottles."

"So anyone who was in the house could have put something into one of them."

"Of course."

"Do we know who visited him – apart from Claudia presumably and Julie before they split up."

"We did try to check on any visitors he may have had, but it's difficult. That house is well set back from the road and neighbours wouldn't be able to see who came and went."

"Very convenient – for Malcolm Hardy, that is."

"But not for us."

"I've just thought of something," I said.

"Yes?"

"When I was in the house with Anthea I happened to go into the larder. The sash cord of the window in there was broken. I didn't notice if the catch was on but it's quite a large window, certainly large enough for someone to climb in, and it's on the ground floor."

"I'll certainly check that."

"Only with all the shrubs and things around it would be quite easy to get in without being seen, especially at night. "

"Quite."

I laughed. "All right, I'll stop stating the obvious and leave you in peace. What were you doing anyway?"

"I was helping Delia with her homework, but as we were involved in a tedious mathematical problem I was probably not going to be able to solve, I was delighted to be called away. I'll let you know what, if anything, we find at the house."

That night I dreamt that I was helping Claudia Drummond climb into the larder of Malcolm Hardy's house in order to turn up the central heating there. But I didn't feel, somehow, that my subconscious was trying to tell me anything important.

Chapter Seventeen

The first real harbinger of Christmas for me is the card I receive from my cousin in Kirkby Lonsdale. I always imagine her sitting watching the clock at midnight on November 30th waiting for it to lurch over into December so that she can start sending out her Christmas cards. The card (a view of Kirkby Lonsdale church in the snow) duly arrived and I nerved myself to go into action. Shopping for presents now assumed an urgency that took away all the pleasure and left only the frustration of not being able to find things even when I'd thought of them. My eye kept being caught by enchanting little woolly animals that I was sure would delight Alice, and I had to exercise extreme self-control and limit myself to three (a lamb, a lion and a rabbit) as well as a small teddy bear wearing a t-shirt with the legend "Somerset: the Team To Watch".

As I approached the post office one morning, I found Rosemary eyeing in dismay the immensely long queue that had threaded its way all round the interior and was now outside in the street.

"Oh goodness," I said. "I don't think I can bear to wait in *that*. I'll have to come back later. I've got to send these today, it's the last day for posting overseas things."

"I don't believe a word of it," Rosemary said. "They only say that to frighten you. I always leave my cards and things until after the final date and they get there much more quickly because everyone's posted early."

I considered this possibly specious reasoning.

"You're probably right," I said, "only I don't think I'm brave enough to try."

"Well," Rosemary said, "it's no use waiting here in the freezing cold, let's go and have a coffee."

Plying me with coffee (and a warming Danish pastry) Rosemary had a favour to ask.

"I was going to ring you, actually. I know it's an awful lot to ask, but do you think you could possibly take some papers round to Mother tomorrow? They're things I had to sign and then she has to sign – you know, accountant's stuff – but it has to be done tomorrow, because they're rather urgent. The thing is, Jack and I simply *have* to go to this wretched lunch (something to do with one of his clients) and it's in Salisbury so we'll have to leave frightfully early and won't get back until heaven knows when."

"Yes of course I will."

"Needless to say I tried to get out of it – *not* my idea of fun – but Jack said I must."

"Salisbury's nice."

"Lovely, but I won't get to see much of it!" She put two lumps of sugar in her coffee and stirred it defiantly. "Yes, I know I shouldn't and I know I'm nearly a stone overweight already, but I do need to keep up my strength!"

"Oh, I've given up worrying about all that – at least until after Christmas. So about the papers, when would you like me to collect them?"

"I won't have them until this evening – quite late when Jack comes back, so if we could drop them off with you on our way tomorrow. As I said, it'll be frightfully early so we won't disturb you, just put them through the letterbox. Then if you could ask

204

Mother to sign them – Jack will have marked the places – and pop them back through *our* letterbox on your way back. Sorry it's so complicated!"

"That's fine, I've been meaning to go and see your mother for ages now."

"I'll ring and let her know you're coming. Will it be morning or afternoon? Sorry, but you know how she is about times and things!"

"Oh, morning I think. About eleven."

"Bless you. That will be a marvellous help!" She sighed. "This Christmas thing gets worse every year. I start off with all sorts of lists, terrifically organised and then after a bit the whole thing simply degenerates into a muddled mess!"

"I wish *I* was more organised," I said ruefully. "I've only done my overseas cards so far, all the rest are lying about in drifts all over my desk. There are times when I positively *resent* the cards that arrive before I've sent out mine. And as for my cousin Margaret sitting smugly up in Kirkby Lonsdale with everything done – well!"

Rosemary laughed, then she said, "Oh, I knew there was something I meant to tell you. Did you know that Malcolm Hardy had a cousin?"

"No! Really?"

"Yes, Mother was telling me about it the other day. She was going on about the murder and so forth and she said that Geraldine Hardy, you know, Malcolm's mother, had a sister."

"I never knew that."

"No, well, she went to live in Scotland, I can't remember where, but right up in the north somewhere, so they lost touch. Anyway, she, the sister that is, had a son, just the one, and when Geraldine died there was some sort of fuss about some heirloom that the sister said should have gone to her. Mother knows the details – of course!"

"Of course!" I said.

"And apparently there's been bad blood between Malcolm and the son (I don't remember his name), especially after *his* mother died."

"How fascinating. Where does Malcolm's cousin live now?"

"Oh, London I think. I gather he's a doctor – not a GP, I don't think – so presumably some sort of consultant and quite grand."

When I arrived at Mrs Dudley's next morning she was very brisk.

"Now," she said, "let's get these papers dealt with straightaway."

Mrs Dudley has always seen herself as 'a good businesswoman' and since in recent years she hasn't had much occasion to demonstrate her powers she wasn't going to let an occasion like this slip away from her. She made great play of getting out another pair of spectacles and putting them on, then she spread the papers over her table while I tactfully went over to the window and looked out at the garden, bare, but (of course) immaculately tidy. However, Mrs Dudley did not intend to be deprived of her audience. Accidentally or on purpose she knocked some of the papers onto the floor so that I had to go over and pick them up.

"Thank you Sheila. Perhaps you would be good enough to put them into sequence for me – the pages are numbered – and then hand them to me one at a time in the right order."

As I handed each page to her she studied it carefully, initialled each one and then, on the final page, as if she was putting her signature to some world-shaking international treaty, she wrote her name with a flourish, gathered up the papers and gave them to me to put back into the envelope. Feeling like some minor Foreign Office official, I did so and she sat back with an air of satisfaction and rang the bell for Elsie to bring in the coffee.

As well as coffee (to be poured by me with some trepidation from the heavy silver coffee pot) there was a plate of Elsie's delicious cinnamon biscuits as well as her homemade shortbread, so I felt well rewarded for my labours. I also thought this might be a good opportunity, while Mrs Dudley was in a mellow mood, of getting some information.

"Rosemary said that Malcolm Hardy had an aunt and a cousin," I said. "I never knew that."

"Oh yes." Mrs Dudley said, pleased, as always, to be in the position of knowing more than somebody else. "Geraldine Hardy – she was Geraldine Miller, you know – had a sister, Dorothy. Their father was a dentist, he had a practice up on West Hill. But *his* father came down here from London and he was, I believe, a very successful businessman, quite well off."

"Really?"

"Unfortunately," Mrs Dudley continued with some satisfaction, "he had this addiction to horse racing and other forms of gambling and lost a great deal of his money so that, in the end, they lived in really quite reduced circumstances."

"How sad."

Mrs Dudley gave me a disapproving glance. "Not sad at all," she said. "Improvident. However, his son trained as a dentist and made quite a good living. He married Esther Nichols and she had some money of her own. They bought that end house on the Porlock Road, just before you get to Bracken, quite a nice property. And both the girls, Geraldine and Dorothy, were good looking enough to make advantageous marriages. Geraldine managed to catch John Hardy after his first wife died and Dorothy married some sort of Scottish lawyer – they call them something different up there I believe – and went to live in the Highlands. Caithness, I believe, or was it Sutherland? In any case, she was not on the spot when their father died – the mother had died some years before – so she was not in a position to see what happened to all his Things." Mrs Dudley gave the last word particular significance. "And that was where she made her mistake."

"Goodness," I said eagerly, "what was that?"

"Well," Mrs Dudley, satisfied at having totally captured my attention, leaned back in her chair, "there was the picture. She didn't know about that."

"The picture?"

"A Victorian painting. The girls had never really cared for it – an undraped female in some sort of classical setting. It had belonged to their grandfather, one of the few things that hadn't been sold, I believe, to pay his gambling debts. "

"Valuable?"

"Oh yes," Mrs Dudley said with some satisfaction. "When Geraldine's father died she had the pick of the furniture and so forth – Dorothy didn't come down for the funeral for some reason and Leonard Hardy, who was always very shrewd, had some of the stuff valued. It turned out that the picture was by some quite famous painter – now what was he called? Sounds like a woman's name but he was a man..."

"Alma Tadema?" I suggested.

"That's the one – such a stupid name – but apparently he was very well known, the Royal Academy and that sort of thing. So the picture turned out to be worth a considerable sum of money. Well, Geraldine, who, as I said didn't care for the painting, wanted to sell it, but Leonard Hardy thought that if they held on to it it would increase in value – and of course he was right. They tell me such things fetch an astonishing amount of money these days."

"Oh they do," I said. "But was it Geraldine's to sell? What about Dorothy?"

Mrs Dudley gave a short laugh. "Dorothy didn't know anything about it," she said. "As far as she knew none of their father's things was worth anything and Geraldine certainly didn't tell her otherwise."

"I see."

"However," Mrs Dudley continued with some relish, "you can't keep that sort of thing quiet for ever. Dorothy found out somehow about the picture – I expect someone felt it their duty to tell her – and, naturally enough, she was extremely angry."

"Didn't their father leave a will?" I asked.

"Oh yes, but that only said that his money should be divided equally between them, and so it was, including the money from the sale of the house – I believe it fetched quite a good price, Francis James and his wife

209

bought it – but nothing was said about who was to have the contents. Of course, most of the stuff was sold, not that one gets a proper price for really good things at a time like that, but, by then Leonard Hardy had had the valuers in and found out about the picture."

"So what happened then?"

"There was a certain amount of bad tempered correspondence between the two girls."

"They didn't go to court about it? I mean, if Dorothy was married to a lawyer..."

"Oh, he'd died by then, he was some years older than she was. No, it's a great mistake getting lawyers mixed up in things, much better to keep these things in the family. All lawyers are dishonest." She gave me one of her rare smiles. "Always excepting dear Michael of course."

She handed me her empty coffee cup to put back on the tray and settled herself back in her chair again. "A little while later," she continued, "Dorothy died and so did Geraldine."

"So there was just Malcolm Hardy left and he got to keep the picture? No, hang on, Rosemary said there was a cousin. Presumably, then, Dorothy had a child."

Mrs Dudley nodded her approval at my deduction. "Exactly," she said. "A boy called Donald."

"So is the feud over the picture still going on? "

"It certainly was when Malcolm Hardy was alive," she said. "What will happen now, of course, I don't know. It may be that June will feel that this man has a right to it. After all it belonged to Geraldine's side of the family and not the Hardys'. It will be her decision."

210

I didn't, naturally, tell Mrs Dudley that it would probably *not* be June's decision, but Julie's, which might be quite different.

"Do you know where this son lives?" I asked. "Is it somewhere in Scotland?"

"No," Mrs Dudley said, "he lives in London. He is a doctor, apparently quite high up in his profession, some kind of specialist I believe."

On the way home I tried to remember if I had seen a picture answering that description at The Willows when Anthea and I were there. I couldn't remember it in any of the downstairs rooms, but then I recalled Mrs Dudley's description of it as 'an undraped female'. It was most likely, then, that it had been in the gallery of similarly undraped females in Malcolm Hardy's bedroom. I hadn't examined the collection in detail since I had been so taken aback by what I saw and with Anthea registering profound disapproval in the doorway it had hardly seemed the moment to make any sort of inventory.

The appearance on the scene, as it were, of one more person who had a reason to dislike Malcolm Hardy might perhaps be said to have added another dimension to the problem of his murder. Had this Donald person (what was his surname?) been in touch with his cousin recently? Even if he had a motive for the murder (and was the picture really motive enough for such a violent act?) how could he have had the opportunity to administer the fatal dose? Indeed, how would he have known what sort of fatal dose was needed?

It seemed, on reflection, that what might have been a promising lead was simply a false trail that would get us nowhere. However, when I saw Rosemary a few days later I couldn't resist asking her if she knew what Donald's surname was.

"Oh, let me see now – Mother did tell me – something Scottish, Macsomething... No," she said triumphantly, "I know. It's Gillespie, Donald Gillespie. Why do you want to know?"

"Your mother told me about the picture and all the bad feeling, so I wondered if there just might have been the faint possibility –"

"That this Gillespie man might have murdered Malcolm Hardy?"

"Well, it *is* a possibility. Not a very strong one, I admit."

"I can't think," Rosemary said, "why you're scratching around for yet another suspect. Surely there are quite enough close to hand without dragging in someone from outside!"

"Yes, I suppose so," I said reluctantly. "The trouble is, I know all the suspects close at hand and I like them all. I'd much rather the murderer was someone from far away who I'd never met and knew nothing about."

"That's not very fair!"

"I know. But you must admit it's difficult to think of anyone at the surgery being a killer. Isn't it?"

"I suppose so." She thought for a moment and then she said, "Still, there's always Claudia Drummond. We don't like *her*."

"Mmm, she is a possibility. But, somehow, suddenly discovering about this cousin, at this stage, and a sort of motive... I wonder what the picture is worth?"

"Who did you say it was by?"

"Alma Tadema."

"Oh yes, I always mix him up with the other one – you know who I mean, the one there was that exhibition of at the Tate a few years ago."

"Lord Leighton?"

"That's right, all that classical stuff, odalisques and so forth."

"There was quite a vogue at that time for langorous ladies lying about on marble benches. And of course there's a tremendous interest in Victorian painting now, people pay vast sums of money for them."

"How vast? Millions, like for those rather dim French things or horrible scribbles by Picasso?"

"Not millions perhaps. Hundreds of thousands, though. I suppose it depends on what size it is and if it's a good example of the genre."

"Enough to commit a murder for?"

"I suppose it would depend how much you needed the money. If this cousin is a successful London consultant he's hardly likely to be short of a bob or two. It would be interesting to know, though, if the picture's still there, at the Willows, I mean."

"You could always ask Roger," Rosemary suggested. "I don't suppose it's an official secret or anything."

"Yes," I said thoughtfully. "I might just do that."

Chapter Eighteen

Egged on by those television advertisements for a certain dry food guaranteed to prolong your cat's active life, I called in at the surgery to see what they had on offer. When I got there Kathy and Julie were at the front desk engaged in what looked like a serious conversation. When they looked up and saw that it was me Kathy said, "Here's the very person. Mrs Malory is a great friend of Chief Inspector Eliot so she'll know if you ought to tell him."

"Tell him what?" I asked.

Julie looked nervously at Kathy and then said reluctantly, "I don't suppose it's all that important and I don't want to go bothering the police. Anyway, it might cause trouble."

"If you know anything, anything at all," I said, "I do think you ought to tell someone."

"Well I think it might be important," Kathy said. "Anyway, why don't you tell Mrs Malory and see if she agrees with me."

"Yes," I said, smiling in what I hoped was an encouraging manner, "tell me what it is and we'll see."

"It was while I was with Malcolm," Julie began hesitantly. "It was at a weekend, late one Sunday morning, we were just going out for a drink and the doorbell went. Malcolm went to the door and I heard him in the hall talking to someone on the doorstep, then he said 'I suppose you'd better come in.' A man came in with him, a bit older than Malcolm I would think. Anyway

Malcolm said to me 'Get lost Julie, I've got some business to see to.' So I went out of the room."

"Did he often speak to you like that?" I asked.

She gave a little shrug. "Sometimes," she said. "This time it made me really annoyed – it was the way he said it, as if I was nobody, just someone to be got out of the way. Well, because I was annoyed I didn't close the door properly and I stayed outside to listen to what they were saying. Malcolm said, 'Look here Gillespie, what do you mean by badgering me at home like this? I told you on the phone that I hadn't got the damned picture.' Then the other man said, 'Where is it then?' and Malcolm said, 'I told you before, my mother got rid of it years ago'. That made the man really angry and he said, 'In that case I want the money – it's rightfully mine.' Malcolm laughed and said, 'You can whistle for the money, Gillespie, you haven't got a leg to stand on. Now get out of my house and if you ever come here again I'll call the police.' They came over to the door so I had to move away fast, but I heard the other man shouting out as he left, 'You haven't heard the last of this – I'll get even with you one way or another.' "

Julie stopped and looked at me enquiringly.

"So what do you think?" she asked. "Should I tell the police?"

"Oh yes," I said, "most certainly. How was Malcolm after the man left?"

"Oh, he was *very* pleased with himself, as if he'd done something clever. I was a bit surprised because it all seemed a bit odd, but then I forgot about it, and I only remembered it when I saw that one of the new reps was called Gillespie, Mike Gillespie he is, but he's young and quite different to the man who called. Still it made me remember and, when you think about that man, it did sound a bit threatening, that last remark of his. So I wondered if he had anything to do with it – you know, the murder."

"I think that's for the police to decide," I said, "but you must certainly tell them, it's something they need to know." I thought for a moment. "Come to think of it, I shall be speaking to Chief Inspector Eliot myself this evening. Would you like me to mention it to him? Then he can get in touch so that you can give him the details."

She smiled gratefully. "Oh that would be kind of you, if you're sure that will be all right."

"Yes of course. Incidentally, how are you after that nasty fall? Is everything all right with the baby?"

"Oh yes, I'm fine and so's the baby. But I'm only working part time now and Keith says I must give up altogether next month and rest properly."

When I got back home Foss began weaving around my legs demanding something to eat so I poured some of the dried food into his dish and put it down for him. He sniffed it cautiously, gave me a look of complete contempt and stalked away. Even Tris, coming in and seeing uneaten food, only managed a couple of mouthfuls before abandoning it in disgust. Oh well, I thought, as I put the rejected food out for the birds, I suppose my visit to the surgery wasn't a complete waste of time since I had gleaned some useful information about Malcolm Hardy and his cousin. And also (the thought occurred to me) confirmation of Keith's extremely protective attitude towards Julie and her baby.

Roger sounded quite interested in what I had to tell him.

"You do seem to attract information like a magnet," he said. "I haven't the least idea whether all this has anything to do with the murder but it's certainly something that should be followed up."

"I suppose you don't know," I said tentatively, "if the picture *is* still in the house. I thought it might be among Malcolm Hardy's gallery of young ladies."

"I'll have to go and have a look," Roger said, "and I expect, Sheila, that you'd like to come with me, wouldn't you?"

"Well, of course..."

"Would tomorrow at two thirty suit you? I'll see you there."

The Willows was even more dank and miserable than the last time I'd been there with Anthea. I wrapped my coat more closely about me although it wasn't the cold that I felt the need to ward off. Roger, however, merely said, "Very bad to keep a place like this shut up for so long. It need a thorough airing," before moving from the hall into the drawing room.

"Do we have any idea of what this picture looks like?" he asked.

"Typical Alma Tadema, I imagine. Victorian classical."

I looked at the pictures on the figured damask wallpaper (sage green to match the hall) which were mostly of heavily wooded landscapes with thatched cottages and small figures engaged in various kinds of rural activities. There were also a couple featuring meditative cows (after the Dutch School) standing in or beside streams and a large still life with baskets of

218

fruit and flowers interspersed with dead ducks, pheasants and the corpse of a particularly realistic wood pigeon which made me look hastily away.

"Nothing like that here," I said, "and it wasn't in the hall so it must be upstairs."

The impact of Malcolm Hardy's picture collection in the bedroom, though not as startling as the first time I saw it, was still disturbing.

"I think they're mostly reproductions," I said, trying to keep my voice casual, as if I encountered such things every day. "Prints or pictures taken from art magazines and framed."

"They all seem to be by famous artists," Roger said. "A very eclectic selection. From Botticelli to Modigliani. But is there an Alma Tadema?"

"There's a reproduction of Canova's Three Graces," I said after a careful search, "but nothing else at all classical."

"You're right it's not here. Perhaps we'd better look in the other rooms up here just in case."

We checked the other bedrooms and the landing with no luck.

"I suppose he might have hidden it away," I suggested. "There's boxes of stuff up in the attics. I mean, if he knew that his cousin was after it he might feel it would be safer if it wasn't on view. Shall we have a look?"

But in spite of much hauling about of dusty tea chests and old trunks we found nothing that resembled the missing picture. The water had been turned off in the bathroom so we weren't able to wash our grubby hands there.

"It may still be on in the kitchen," Roger said. "Let's go and see."

There was water there and when we were reasonably clean again Roger said, "I'll just go and check that window you mentioned in the larder."

He moved across and switched on the light.

"Oh yes, broken sash cord, as you said." He gave the window a tug and after a couple of tries it opened. "And no lock on it."

He pulled the window right up and looked out.

"Several bushes out here, good cover if you wanted to break in without being seen."

"Do you think anyone did break in there?"

"Don't know. The window's very stiff, but it could be done. Not a burglar though, well, not a burglar as such, since nothing seems to be missing."

"Except the picture."

"As you say."

"Do you think the cousin did break in and steal it?" I asked.

"I'd need to get forensics down here to check the window and the ground underneath it. I really don't know."

"And do you think it had anything to do with Malcolm Hardy's death?"

"I would be obliged, Sheila," Roger said with a smile, "if you wouldn't keep asking me questions to which I do not have the answers!"

"It does seem odd though, doesn't it, that this cousin should appear just before Malcolm Hardy died."

"Possibly."

"And he is a doctor so he could easily have got hold of the insulin."

"True."

"But you don't think he had anything to do with it?"

"Let's put it this way. How would he have known about Malcolm Hardy's condition and the medication he'd been taking? And if he didn't know about that then he couldn't be the murderer."

"No," I agreed sadly. "I don't suppose he could. *Unless*," I said, struck by a sudden thought, "he'd been in touch with another member of the family – June Hardy perhaps – who *might* have said something to him that might have suggested Malcolm's condition, and, being a doctor, he might have deduced what sort of medication was being used to treat it!"

"Might, might, might! Come on, Sheila that's really fantasy-land!"

"Well," I said stubbornly, "I could just have a word with June, to see if she's heard from this Gillespie man."

"I fear you will be wasting your time."

We went back along the passage into the hall.

"Hang on," Roger said. "We didn't check his study."

But there was no Alma Tadema lurking among the modern art on the cream-covered walls.

"No," I said, "It's not here. I think it must have gone."

Roger was standing looking around him.

"It's funny, you know," he said, "but I can't help feeling that there's something here that we've missed."

I looked about me at the fancy wallpaper and the trendy furniture but nothing suggested itself to me. My eye fell on the drinks trolley.

"I suppose the whisky in his flask came from one of these bottles," I said.

"It seems likely, but we did check them and there were no traces of any other substance in them."

"Were they checked here?"

"Yes, I believe so. Actually, I didn't read the report myself – I was out of town at the time it came through. My sergeant gave me the gist. "

"I just wondered if the bottles had been tested for fingerprints."

"I imagine so – why?"

"Well, it did occur to me that anyone – not just the cousin – could have got through that window and put something in the bottles, or in the hip flask for that matter if it was lying about near the bottles, which it could have been, and they might have wiped one of the bottles clean."

"I think my sergeant would have noticed if that had happened."

"Yes, of course. But you do agree that someone could have got in through the larder window."

"Yes. As I said, I'll have forensics go over it thoroughly."

"Of course, Julie might still have a key. I know she'd never actually moved in with him, but she must have been in and out of here quite a bit."

"I did ask her and she said she'd never had one. I don't think Malcolm Hardy was in the habit of trusting anyone, even his girlfriend."

"No, and after that row they had... oh well, I can't think of anyone else who might have had access to the place. Unless there was a cleaning woman – I mean, there would have to be someone with a house this size, surely?"

"He had a commercial firm in once a week, three people who went through the place while he was here. Like I said, he didn't seem to have trusted anyone.

Even the gardener was never allowed into the actual house."

I sighed and looked round the room once again. There was something vaguely unpleasant about it – even more unpleasant, in a way, than the bedroom. It seemed wrong, shocking almost, to have taken this room and wrenched it, as it were, out of context. The fact that he had left the drawing room exactly as it was in his father's day merely emphasised his scorn for the taste of the previous generation. *Look at me*, it seemed to say, *and see how far I have come from that dreary lot, how smart and modern I am and how tedious and dull they were.*

"What is it, Sheila?" Roger asked. "You were scowling horribly!"

I laughed. "I suppose I was just thinking how ephemeral taste is. In a few years' time this will be even more old fashioned than that room next door."

He laughed and moved back again to the drinks trolley, examining the whisky bottles absently. He unscrewed the cap of one of them and sniffed the contents.

"Good stuff this. Whatever else you might say about him he certainly knew his whisky."

He unscrewed another and sniffed that. Then he sniffed it again.

"That's odd," he said.

"What?"

"The Glenfiddich. "

He took a glass, poured a little whisky into it and drank it.

"That's not a single malt."

"So?"

"Why would Malcolm Hardy have a cheap blended whisky in a Glenfiddich bottle?"

"Perhaps he was just mean and gave that one to his visitors and kept the best stuff for himself."

"I don't think so. Someone who had a display of drinks like this would want to show off to any visitor."

"So what do you think?"

"I think," Roger said, "I'd like this particular bottle examined more carefully for fingerprints."

"Really?"

He looked about him

"Now what can I put it in?"

"I've got a plastic carrier bag in my handbag," I said.

"Good heavens, women are so extraordinary. What on earth do you carry that about for?"

"Oh," I said vaguely, "just in case – you know."

Roger put the whisky bottle carefully in the carrier bag.

"I knew," he said, "that there was *something* about this room!"

A couple of days later I was making some mince pies – I always like to have some made well before Christmas to give to anyone who might drop in. I'd just got the pastry rolled out when the phone rang. It was Roger.

"I thought you'd like to know," he said. "I've had the lab report on that Glenfiddich bottle. It was some sort of cheap blended stuff, but that's not the interesting thing."

"Oh?"

"It was in the original report but it somehow got

overlooked. Anyway, they have confirmed that the fingerprints on the bottle are blurred."

"What does that mean?"

"It means that someone handled that bottle wearing gloves. And I think it seems likely that whoever handled the bottle put the cheap whisky in it."

"And?"

"And, it's possible that whoever it was put more than whisky into that bottle."

I returned to the mince pies but my mind was in such a whirl that I put too much mincemeat in them and it all oozed out over the edges and they were quite spoilt.

Chapter Nineteen

I saw June Hardy at the Hospital Friends meeting a few days later. I thought she was looking very tired, but when the meeting was over and everyone was moving across to the side table to get a cup of coffee she was making for the door. I caught up with her and said, "Are you all right June, you look thoroughly exhausted."

She gave me a slight smile and said, "I was up most of last night with Mrs Hewlett. She had a stroke so we had to call the doctor and get her into hospital. I'm just on my way to see her now."

"Oh, do spare a few minutes to have a coffee. You really look as if you need it!"

She hesitated for a moment, looked at her watch and then said, "Very well. I must say I could do with a bit of a break."

"You go and sit down there over by the window," I said, "and I'll get the coffees."

I put the cups of coffee on the window sill and said "I'm so sorry about Mrs Hewlett. Is she going to be all right?"

"Yes, I think so. It wasn't a very severe stroke, but I was afraid she might go on to have a second one – it happens sometimes as you know and then that can be serious."

"But she didn't?"

"No, thank goodness. But naturally I'll feel happier when I've seen her.

"Of course." I took a sip of my coffee which, as

usual, didn't taste of anything in particular but was warm and comforting. "They're so lucky to have you in charge," I said. "You do a wonderful job."

"I enjoy doing it – I suppose it's my life really. They are like a family to me, now that I have none of my own."

"Oh yes," I said casually, as if I'd just thought of it, "that reminds me. Someone said that Malcolm's cousin – a Donald Gillespie, is that right? – was in Taviscombe recently. Do you know him at all?"

"Good heavens! I haven't heard anything about him for a very long time."

"Apparently he went to call on Malcolm."

"That does surprise me. There was no love lost there!"

"Really?"

"There was some quarrel about a picture – I don't know the ins and outs of it, but it was all very unpleasant."

"Did you know Donald Gillespie at all?"

"Oh no, I never had anything to do with *her* side of the family. And, of course, I was away in Bristol for many years."

"Yes, of course, so you were."

June hesitated for a moment and then she said, "Sheila, I believe you know the Inspector in charge of the investigation into Malcolm's death. Has there been any progress, only it does seem to have been a long time since it happened. Do they have any idea who might have done it?"

"I don't know," I said, not being sure how much I could reveal. "I believe they've got a few leads, but I don't think they're expecting to make an arrest or anything."

"I see. Presumably they will tell me when there is anything to tell, since I am his next of kin –" She broke off and thought for a moment and then she continued, "Or, at least I suppose I am, though this girl, this Julie – her baby will be that no doubt, when it is born."

"She very nearly lost it," I said. "Did you hear?"

June looked startled. "What happened?"

I told her about the accident at Dunster. "But she's all right now, and the baby. I saw them recently and she seemed fine. In fact she was the person who told me about Donald Gillespie calling to see Malcolm."

"Really?" June looked at her watch. "Good gracious, is that the time? I must be getting on if I want to see Mrs Hewlett. They have lunch just *before* twelve on Bratton Ward. It's been nice talking to you, Sheila, and you were right, the cup of coffee was just what I needed."

When she had gone I sat for a little while longer, looking down at the people hurrying by in the street below. The Christmas decorations were already up and from above the scene looked quite festive.

"Nearly Christmas already," Mr Mortimer said, coming up and joining me at the window. "It seems like only yesterday we were organising the summer fete. I really don't know where this year has gone! Now are you sure we have enough volunteers to provide the food after the carol concert – a lot of people are down with this flu bug, you know, so there may be some problems."

When I left the hospital I didn't feel like going home to prepare a solitary lunch so I went into the Buttery to get a quick snack. I'd just settled down to my ham roll and coffee when a voice said, "Hello, Mrs Malory, can I join you?" It was Ben Turner's daughter Tina.

"Yes, of course. How nice to see you. How's your little boy, William, isn't it?"

"He's fine," Tina said, putting her tray down on the table. "He's with my mother-in-law this afternoon, she has him sometimes to give me a break."

"That's nice."

"I'm going to see my mother after I've had lunch. She's been ill lately, I mean as well as the Alzheimers."

"I'm so sorry."

"It's her heart you see." She ate a little of her quiche and then pushed it to one side and said earnestly, "I just wish she could slip away, die quickly. Isn't that awful? To think such a thing about your own mother!"

"Not really," I said. "My own mother suffered a lot at the end of her life and there were many times when I felt as you do."

She gave me a grateful smile. "She has no sort of life really, especially now that she's so weak, and it's so awful for my father."

"I can imagine. I was so glad, by the way, to hear that he's staying on at the practice."

"Yes, thank goodness. But, oh I do wish things could come right for him."

"Come right?"

She hesitated for a moment and then she said, "I shouldn't be telling you this, but he's in love with someone and of course they can't be together with the situation as it is."

"You knew?"

She looked at me in surprise. "*You* knew?" she asked, "about him and Kathy?"

"Kathy did confide in me," I said. "She hadn't

230

anyone else she could tell – she felt her parents wouldn't understand. I know she feels terrible about it, because of your mother. How do *you* feel about it?"

Tina stirred her coffee thoughtfully. "I think I'm glad for him. He's had so much misery, I'm pleased he's found someone who can make him happy."

"That's very generous of you," I said.

"I love my mother, but I love my father more and, quite honestly, it can't affect her now so what does it matter."

"I think you should tell them that," I said. "They've been terrified you might find out and be hurt. Incidentally, how did you find out?"

Tina smiled. "My father is very transparent. He couldn't help mentioning her from time to time and – well, I found a letter. I know I shouldn't have read it, but I did. She obviously loves him very much."

"They're both good people, you know."

"I know."

"So please do tell them that you know and that you understand. It would mean so much to them."

She nodded. "If you think it would help then I'll talk to my father."

"Thank you."

"At least things seem to be better at the surgery now that that dreadful man isn't there. Do they have any idea yet who killed him?"

I shook my head. "I don't think so."

"Well," Tina said finishing off her quiche with a better appetite. "I hope they don't catch whoever it is who did it – the world's a better place without him!"

That did seem to be the general opinion and I heard it echoed by Kathy when I went round to see her. I couldn't resist telling her about my conversation with Tina so that evening I'd telephoned to ask if I could come round.

"It's nice to see you Sheila," Kathy said as she welcomed me in. "Ben had a call from his daughter saying she wanted to see him this evening so I'm on my own. I don't know why she wants to see him – I suppose it's about her mother. Poor Ben, it's so difficult for him, he hates deceiving people."

"Well," I said, "at least he won't have to deceive Tina any longer." And I told her about my conversation that lunchtime.

"I know I should have waited to let Ben tell you," I said, "and you mustn't let him know that I told you, but I couldn't resist, I was so pleased and excited for you. I do hope you don't mind."

"No, no, of course not, I'm so pleased, so *relieved*! Do you think that's what Tina wants to talk to him about tonight?"

"I expect so."

"Oh thank you, Sheila!"

"Don't thank me. I didn't do anything."

"Yes you did. If you hadn't spoken to her like that she might never have told Ben that it was all right."

"Well, if you think I did some good I'm very glad."

"Of course we won't let anyone else know – it wouldn't be fair. But it was Tina who was worrying us. It was Tina that Malcolm threatened to tell. That hateful man – I'm glad he's dead after all that he put us through. Oh if only we'd *known*!" She was almost in tears.

"Don't think about any of that now," I said. "Just

enjoy the fact that you can be happy together without feeling guilty."

I stayed a little while with Kathy and when I got home I found myself thinking about what she had said. If only they'd known – what? Kathy had been so vehement, so upset when she spoke about it. Had they decided to silence Malcolm Hardy so that he couldn't reveal their secret? I could hardly bear to consider that possibility, especially now that things seemed to be coming right for them at last. It would be dreadful if there were to be no happy ending. But the fact remained that they both had the means and the opportunity (not to mention the motive) to kill Malcolm Hardy.

I poured myself a glass of wine – Kathy had offered me something but I'd refused, not wanting to be there when Ben arrived with his good news – and settled myself on the sofa. The animals, who had consumed their tribute of food in the kitchen, came and joined me as I thought once more about Malcolm Hardy's death. Of course, I told myself, the discovery that Roger had made about the whisky made it seem most likely that it was from that bottle the hip flask had been filled and that's where the insulin had been. Therefore, I thought, it meant that the people at the surgery were all in the clear – Kathy and Ben and Diana and Keith and, probably, Julie. That only left Claudia, who would almost certainly have been in the house at some point during their affair, and the cousin, Donald Gillespie, who we knew had called at least once and might very well have called again.

I sat there mechanically stroking Foss's head and

trying to work out which of those two was most likely to be the murderer and if, indeed, either of them had sufficient motive to resort to murder. I suppose motive is relative. What might be a powerful enough reason for one person to commit a crime might not be sufficient for another. Did Claudia care enough about her marriage to worry if Malcolm Hardy, in a fit of fury at being rejected, told her husband about their affair? Was Donald Gillespie sufficiently obsessed about the picture and the wrong he felt had been done to his mother, or did he need money so desperately that he would risk killing his cousin? Since I didn't actually know the two people concerned I had no way of telling.

"But then..." I said out loud, causing Tris to wake suddenly and look at me in surprise,

"...but then there's the larder window." Tris lowered his head onto his paws again and I continued my thoughts in silence. The larder window, which might have provided a way for the murderer to get into the house, threw the whole thing wide open again. It meant that anyone, people from the surgery too, might have got into the house to put the insulin in the whisky bottle. Well, perhaps not anyone. Presumably Julie, whatever her stage of pregnancy, wouldn't have been rash enough to go climbing through windows. And who would have known about the window anyway? I very much doubted if anyone from the practice would have been invited to the house. Possibly the murderer might have prowled around when Malcolm Hardy was away (it would be easy enough to do that without being seen) and discovered the window by chance.

The telephone rang, causing Foss to leap suddenly off my lap, digging his claws in as he went.

"Sheila." It was Roger. "Sorry to ring you so late, but I thought you might like to know that forensics have said that no one got in through that larder window. There were absolutely no traces at all."

"Oh," I said flatly.

"And really," he continued, "it was *very* stiff – I had to really shove it to get it open. I expect that's why they didn't consider it worth mentioning in their report in the first place."

"Yes, I see."

"You sound very disappointed."

"I am rather. It did seem a possibility."

"Well, you can't be right every time."

"So where does it leave us?"

"There wasn't any sign of a forced entry, so the person who put the insulin in the whisky must have been invited into the house by Malcolm Hardy himself."

"Julie, Claudia, the cousin?" I suggested. "Though I suppose if someone from the practice arrived on the doorstep he'd have invited them in. They could perfectly well have invented a plausible excuse for calling."

"Which leaves the field wide open again," Roger said. "I can see we'll have to go right back to first principles and start all over again."

"Not quite *right* back," I said. "Not now you've found out about the whisky being changed, and the hip flask and everything."

Roger sighed. "Not necessarily," he said. "All those things are just possibilities. The insulin could still have

235

been administered in the black coffee by someone at the surgery. The whole thing is still wide open."

"But the different whisky?" I persisted.

"There could be other explanations for that. He could perfectly well have filled up an empty Glenfiddich bottle with a cheaper kind – perhaps to catch someone out – I don't know, but he *could* have done that himself."

"But what about the blurred fingerprints on the bottle?" I asked.

There was a moment's silence then Roger said, "He might have come in from outside and still been wearing his gloves when he picked up the bottle. It is winter, after all, and people do wear gloves."

"Oh, come on Roger, you don't believe that!"

"I really don't know what to believe at the moment," he said.

"And, as we said," I continued, "even if Malcolm did let someone in and they put something in the bottle, they'd still have had to get back into the house after he was dead to change the whisky."

Roger groaned. "Don't, Sheila," he said, "please don't remind me how complicated things are! I'm beginning to think that this murder couldn't have happened, or that it was suicide after all."

"Not possible."

"I suppose not, but wouldn't it be nice if it could be?"

In the silence that followed this remark I heard a wailing sound over the telephone and Roger said, "Oh dear that's Alex. I'm babysitting – it's Jilly's yoga night. I'd better go. Don't stay awake all night trying to puzzle things out!"

After such an eventful day I was really tired and so I didn't stay awake brooding about the Hardy case. Still, just before I fell asleep I heard in my head Kathy's voice saying 'If only we'd *known*!'

Chapter Twenty

If ever you feel the urge to buy a picturesque country cottage, don't, I implore you, be seduced by the picture postcard qualities of a thatched roof. Slate, yes; tiles, admirable; but thatch – no. You might just as well pour all your money down the nearest drain. The temptation, when you've just had it "done" is to look at the neat, golden surface and think "well that's it", but it isn't, because in no time at all one bit or another will become thin, ragged and generally deplorable and you'll have to call the thatcher in all over again. This isn't helped by the depredations of the surrounding wildlife. Squirrels, of course, and woodpeckers are a particular menace. I used to know, when I saw Peter jumping up and down, shaking his fists and shouting with rage, that one of our local woodpeckers had deserted the adjacent telegraph pole and was seeking bigger and better insects in our thatch, pulling out the straw with careless abandon.

Our thatcher, Jim, is almost at retiring age, but fortunately he has an assistant who we hope will carry on the business. Luke is one of those young men who have retired from the rat race (he used to work in a bank) to work at a Craft in the countryside. There are an increasing number of such idealists who have exchanged city offices for run-down old cottages where they set up as potters, blacksmiths and so forth. Actually Luke is a very good thatcher and totally dedicated to his work. I used to worry about him up on the roof in all winds and weathers, his hands and arms red and sore from banging the sections of thatch into place, but he is obviously blissfully happy doing it.

A sweet, very innocent person, he is a vegetarian and passionate about conservation and wildlife. I always remember how horrified he was when he first saw Foss meditatively chewing the head of a baby rabbit he'd caught.

"Does he often do that?" he asked anxiously.

I tried to explain to him about Nature being red in tooth and claw, but although he made a fuss of Foss and stroked him (one of God's creatures after all) I could see he was profoundly disappointed in him.

The day he arrived to re-thatch a section of the roof was fortunately fine and he unloaded the straw from his pick-up truck in a great pile. Tris decided this was a haven for rats and crouched beside it hopefully, while Foss leapt onto the top, regarding it (I saw with a sinking heart) as a good vantage point to leap out at unwary blackbirds.

"I'm afraid the wheat straw wasn't too good this year," Luke said as I took him out a cup of (herbal) tea. "So I'm having to use Polish rye."

"Oh well," I said, "as long as it keeps the rain out!"

Luke gave me a perfunctory smile though he obviously thought I wasn't taking the subject seriously.

I left him and the animals to their various activities and went out. I had a few things I had to do at the post office and the bank so it was quite late in the morning when I finally got into the supermarket. It was one of those mornings when practically every person I know seemed to be shopping there as well, so my progress was slow and when I finally got to the checkout I found the person behind me was June Hardy.

"Hello," I said, "everyone seems to be shopping today!"

"What? Oh yes," she said absently, thrusting her purchases into the carrier bags.

Most unusually she seemed flustered and uncertain so I felt I should help her take things out to the car.

"Are you all right?" I asked as she opened the boot of her old blue Renault and put the packages away.

"Yes, perfectly all right really, it's just that I need to be back at The Larches – the chiropodist is coming just after lunch and I do like to make sure that all the people on the list have remembered and are ready for him. But I seem to have got so behindhand today. Do forgive me, Sheila, if I dash off now – thank you so much for your help..."

She got into the car and drove away before I could reply.

"Was that June?" Anthea had come up beside me. "I wanted to have a word with her about the carol concert at the hospital."

"Yes, she was in a bit of a hurry, I think. She seemed in rather a state, which is not like her at all."

"I know," Anthea agreed. "I thought that when I saw her last week at the opticians. She had one of her old people in tow as usual – she really does too much. I thought she looked very tired."

"That place and those old people are her life, I suppose. But yes, I think she's been overdoing it."

"And all this business about Malcolm Hardy's death and then the will – "

"It must all have been a strain," I agreed, not wishing to enter into any discussion of Malcolm Hardy's will since I wasn't sure how much Anthea knew about it.

"That house!" Anthea said. "I still can't get over it!"

"It was weird," I agreed.

"Downright disgraceful, if you ask me. But I suppose we shouldn't be surprised – such a disagreeable young man. Very like his mother in many ways – Geraldine was always very difficult."

"Did you know her sister Dorothy at all?" I asked, hoping for possible new information. "Or Dorothy's son, Donald?"

"No, they lived somewhere in Scotland, right up in the north, a place no one's heard of. Though I believe the son went to live in London. Why?"

"No reason. Anyway, I must dash. I don't know where this morning's gone."

When I got back home a fine rain was falling though Luke was still on the roof pulling out the old thatch which fell in dusty heaps onto the flower bed below.

"Oh Luke, " I called up, "you're getting so wet. Do come down and have a hot drink or something."

"I'll just finish this bit, Mrs Malory, and then I'll come and have my sandwiches."

"All right, but do come and have a cup of something when you're ready."

It was always tacitly understood that Luke preferred to eat his lunch (some sort of salad sandwich I thought and an organic yoghurt) sitting on a seat in the front porch, though he would allow himself to be coaxed into the kitchen for a cup of something, rather like a timid animal venturing into unfamiliar territory.

I had finished my own lunch and had the kettle on when he appeared in the doorway.

"Do come in," I said, indicating a row of cartons.

"What would you like, peppermint, elderflower or camomile?"

"Oh, camomile please, Mrs Malory, that would be lovely."

He took off his wet donkey jacket and hung it carefully on a hook behind the door. I made the tea for him and coffee for me and we sat and talked cosily for a while. He never tired of telling me how wonderful it was being a thatcher, how good it felt handling natural materials, how good to work out in the fresh air instead of in a centrally heated office.

"But so cold at this time of the year!" I said.

"Very healthy. I like to feel the wind."

"I can't think how you can work that high up."

Luke used ladders and not scaffolding and walked across the roof on a series of boards with prongs that he drove into the thatch.

"I love being high up above the world. It's a funny thing, you know, how people never look up; they're always so busy looking straight ahead or down at their feet, they miss so much."

He broke off to sip his camomile tea. Luke was a great one for telling me little anecdotes to illustrate some semi-philosophical point he wanted to make. "For example," he went on, "a funny thing happened a while ago. I was working on a house in West Street. It was not a very nice day and there weren't many people about, but I heard a car stop and a lady got out and went round the corner to that big house in Holloway Road."

"The Willows?" I asked, startled.

"Is that what it's called? It's the big one on the corner. Anyway, she seemed very anxious not to be seen, looking around her before she went into the drive. Not that anyone *could* have seen her from the road though I could see the house and all the grounds from where I was – you see, that's what I mean, she didn't look up."

He stopped, obviously pleased to have made his point.

"But what happened next?" I asked.

"Oh, she just let herself into the house."

"With a key?"

"Yes. I thought that was funny – I mean, if she had a key why was she being so secretive?"

"She had a key to the front door?"

"Oh no, she went into a door at the side."

I was silent for a moment then I said, "You don't happen to remember when this happened, do you?"

"Well, as a matter of fact I do. It was October the eighth – I know it was then because that was the day I had to finish early because I was going to Taunton that evening; someone had given me a ticket for a folk concert at the Brewhouse. It was quite good, though of course a lot of the stuff is very commercialised nowadays."

He put his mug back on the table and got up.

"Thank you for the tea, Mrs Malory. I'll just get those spars cut while it's raining."

"Luke," I said as he was putting on his jacket. "What did the lady look like – the one who went into The Willows?"

He thought for a moment. "Ordinary looking, really. Middle-aged. Nothing special about her."

"And what sort of car was she driving?"

"Oh dear, I'm not very good at cars. It was an old

one – blue, I think." He looked at me curiously. "Excuse me asking, but why do you want to know?"

"You've helped me solve a mystery."

"Oh," he said, obviously still mystified but not wishing to seem impolite. "I see."

I gave myself the rest of that day and a very disturbed night before I did anything, then I got out the car and drove to The Larches. Nowadays residential homes all have security systems so that you have to wait to be let in. As I stood there waiting I looked around and admired the trim flowerbeds, now planted with winter-flowering pansies and heathers, the seats where in summer the residents could sit out of doors under the trees, the fresh paintwork and the bright curtains at the windows, and I thought what a good job June had done. One of the care workers let me in and I asked if I could see Miss Hardy.

"I think she's free – I'll just pop along and see, if you wouldn't mind waiting here. What name shall I say?"

"Malory, Mrs Malory."

There were comfortable chairs in the hall and several large vases of flowers giving the place a cheerful air.

The care worker reappeared and said, "If you'd like to come this way, Mrs Malory," ushering me into June's office.

It was a pleasant room with french windows leading out into the gardens. The walls and paintwork were white, and on this bright winter's morning seemed to flood the room with light. June was sitting at a large desk but she got up when I came into the room and, motioning me to a large, chintz-covered sofa, sat down beside me.

"Sheila, what a pleasant surprise," she said. "Maisie, would you bring some coffee please."

"No, really, not for me," I said. "Thank you all the same."

June nodded and Maisie left the room.

"Now then," June said. "What can I do for you?"

Somehow I hadn't actually worked out what I was going to say to June, my thoughts had been so confused, so I simply burst out, "I know *how* you did it – what I simply can't understand is *why*!"

Not surprisingly I suppose June looked at me in bewilderment.

"Sheila, what are you talking about?"

"Malcolm Hardy – his murder. I know that you did it."

June, who had been leaning towards me on the sofa, drew back. She had gone perfectly white.

"Malcolm, yes. You say you know?"

"Someone saw you going into The Willows, letting yourself in by the side door with a key."

"But there was no one –" she broke off.

"My thatcher was doing a job just around the corner, he was up on the roof there – you didn't see him, but he saw you."

"I see."

She sat, upright, her hands folded in her lap.

"The police know that the insulin was in that whisky bottle," I said. "Once that was established then anyone's alibi for the day he died was irrelevant."

"What I don't understand," June said, "is how he came to die at the surgery. It was meant to happen at home."

"He filled a hip flask from that bottle of whisky and drank it while he was at work."

"If it had been at home," June said calmly, "when he was all alone, it would have seemed like an accident and no one would have been blamed or suspected. It could have happened at any time. It was quite by chance that I had what you call an alibi."

This unemotional analysis of what had happened took me aback and for a moment I simply looked at her in silence. Then I asked, "But June, *why* did you kill him?"

She looked at me in surprise. "For the money of course."

"The money? But you –"

"Not for me," she broke in impatiently. "For The Larches."

"I don't understand."

"The Larches, it's going to be sold. A company based in the Middle East is buying up residential and nursing homes in the south-west. I couldn't let that happen here."

"But surely – "

"Oh yes, it would be properly run, conforming to standards and so forth, but it wouldn't be the same for my old people. I've seen the new proposals – run to a budget, all for profit. Even if they'd let me stay on – which they wouldn't – they're bringing in new, young people; it wouldn't be possible for things to stay as they are. All the personal touches, knowing people's little ways, giving them small treats and *caring* for them as people not some sort of commodity! They are my family, Sheila, I couldn't let something like that happen to them!"

"Oh, June!"

"Part of that money was mine anyway – Father

should have left me a proper inheritance. What did Malcolm do with it? You saw what he did to the house – disgusting. He had no sense of what was right, he led an immoral life, he made many people unhappy. I had absolutely no qualms about getting rid of him. I knew about his medical condition, of course, and I knew how relatively easy it would be to combine insulin (old Mr Freeman is a diabetic so there is insulin on the premises) with his medication to produce the required result. The locks on the main doors to The Willows have long since been changed, but they didn't bother with the side door – I don't suppose they ever used it – and I still had a key to that."

Her colour was back to normal now. She spoke eagerly, as if she'd wanted for some time to tell someone what she was telling me, but in a strange way now I didn't want to hear it.

"I went to the house when I knew Malcolm would be at the surgery and put the insulin in the whisky. He died a few days later. As soon as the police had finished looking at the house I went back and emptied the bottle, washed it out and put some other whisky in it. I wore gloves, which is, I believe, what criminals do."

"It was the other whisky that gave it away," I said. "It was a blended one, not a single malt."

June made an impatient gesture. "I don't know about such things," she said. "I don't drink spirits."

"But," I said, "you won't get the money after all. Or were you going to kill Julie too?"

"Of course not, what do you take me for!" She was silent for a moment. "Nevertheless, there was a moment when I heard that the girl had nearly miscarried... Sheila, that was dreadful. I really hoped, just for a

248

moment, that that poor innocent child would never be born."

She closed her eyes, as if overcome by some strong emotion. Then she went on, "That's when I knew that I would have to tell the police what I had done."

"You're going to –"

"Just as soon as I have finished making what arrangements I can for my old people. There is not a lot I can do, but I must prepare them as best I can. I have arranged that those with no close relatives shall go to West Lodge; they will be all right there, it is very well run. Those with relatives will be able to make any new arrangements they think fit."

She leaned forward earnestly. "You do understand, don't you, Sheila, that I have to do this? It will take about a week to finalise things. Then, I promise you that I will do as I intended and go to the police."

There was a knock on the door and Maisie put her head round. "Sorry to interrupt Miss Hardy, Dr Macdonald is here to take a look at Mrs Fortescue and you said you wanted to have a word with him before he did."

June got up from the sofa. "Yes, of course, Maisie, I'll be along in just a minute."

I got up too. There seemed nothing more to say. I still found it incredible that June – reliable, upright, *good* June – could have done such a thing, and in such a calculating way. But then, brought up as she had been in such austere and unloving circumstances, I suppose she'd given all her love to the old people in her care, her "family", and she was prepared to do anything, anything at all, to protect them. I could understand that.

"That will be all right then, Sheila?" June said.

"Yes," I replied. "It will be all right."

I was in the toy shop buying just one more thing for Alice's Christmas stocking when I saw Kathy. She was looking at a group of teddy bears.

"Hullo," I said, "aren't they sweet!"

"I was wondering whether to buy one for Tina's little boy," Kathy said. "She's invited Ben and me to lunch on Boxing Day. Though I expect he's already got one."

"No child," I said firmly, "can have too many teddy bears." Kathy laughed, a laugh, I was glad to note, of pure joy. "Isn't Christmas lovely!" she said.

"I *do* love Christmas," Thea said as we were all decorating the Christmas tree. "Absolutely everything about it – commercialism and all!"

Alice, who was trying to pull herself up against the bars of her playpen gave a crow of delight as she finally managed to stand upright, and we all laughed. Michael, unpacking the ornaments from a box, held up two of them so that they sparkled in the light.

"Look Alice!" he said. "Look at the pretty reindeer!"